Wes was ⟨...⟩ and Posy wanted to move him off the ball, but her elbow connected with his stomach. Ashamed that she'd let her frustration toward her mom bleed onto her game, she immediately paused to apologize.

He stole the basketball from her and put it in the hoop, obliterating her small lead. He hadn't even noticed that she hit him, despite the fact that her elbow stung from the contact.

Posy almost called time out. She'd been apologizing for being too big, too rough, *too much* her whole life. Over and over she'd gotten the message that she was too competitive. People got angry when she didn't keep herself in check.

Wes pumped his fist and pointed at her. "You done?"

No. No, she was most definitely not done. She was just getting started.

Dear Reader,

Every time I start a book, one scene cracks it open for me, showing me the characters and helping to shape their story. For Wes Fallon and Posy Jones, that scene was their first encounter on the basketball court. Until I wrote their game, I didn't realize Posy was afraid to be her authentic self or how deep her longing was to find a guy who'd love her just the way she was. From the second Posy gave Wes a shove that was a bit too hard and then immediately felt uncomfortable in her own skin, she became one of my favorite heroines. I wanted her to win. (And not only at basketball.)

Out of Bounds is about characters who aren't sure they're lovable. From Posy, the heroine who suspects she's too intense for a relationship; to Wes, who got shuffled through too many homes as a kid and never understood why; to Angel, the poodle-mix with the heart of an anarchist, these characters struggled to trust. I hope you'll enjoy reading their story as much as I enjoyed writing it.

Extras including behind-the-scenes info, deleted scenes and details about my other books are on my website: www.ellenhartman.com. I blog with the Harlequin Superromance authors at www.superauthors.com, and I'm on Facebook. Send email to ellen@ellenhartman.com. I'd love to hear from you!

Happy reading!

Ellen Hartman

Out of Bounds

ELLEN HARTMAN

HARLEQUIN®

entertain, enrich, inspire™

Recycling programs
for this product may
not exist in your area.

ISBN-13: 978-0-373-71801-6

OUT OF BOUNDS

ABOUT THE AUTHOR

Ellen graduated from Carnegie Mellon with a degree in creative writing and then spent the next fifteen years writing technical documentation. Eventually, she worked up the courage to try fiction and has since published eight novels with Harlequin Superromance. Currently, Ellen lives in a college town in New York with her husband and sons.

Books by Ellen Hartman

HARLEQUIN SUPERROMANCE

Other titles by this author available in ebook format.

This book is dedicated to my editor, Victoria Curran. Who better to receive the dedication in a book about a beloved younger brother than the person who came closest to convincing me that Sam was the more worthy Winchester?

I've learned so much from Victoria about writing stories that keep people entertained.
Being a writer has a lot of perks, working with her is one of my favorites.

CHAPTER ONE

"You said they were bluffing. You said the trade threat was a tactic to get Gary Krota to sign for less money."

Wes slumped on the concrete steps outside his building, the sandwich he'd been planning to eat before practice forgotten next to him. The midday Madrid traffic snarl in the street barely registered. "I told Fabi to ignore the news," he added, "that I was definitely not being traded to Serbia."

A small dog covered in tangled, grayish fur that probably should have been white, nosed into a paper bag lying on the sidewalk. Wes watched it give the bag an investigatory lick.

"That's what I thought," Vic said, his tone flat, and not because it was 6:00 a.m. in the New York agent's office. He'd been negotiating with the owners of the Madrid Pirates, Wes's basketball team, for a week and it was clear he was out of alternatives. Victor hated to lose almost as much as Wes did. "Your option clause lets them trade you, Wes. I have another call set up for later this afternoon, but it's not looking good."

The dog shook the bag.

Wes rubbed a hand across the back of his neck, his fingers glancing against his newly healed shoulder. If he hadn't torn his rotator cuff would he be having this conversation? His numbers had been a little off, but it was a long season. He'd never been a superstar, but was he actually disposable?

"Look, Victor, nothing against Serbia, but I can still contribute here. My shoulder is one hundred percent. Practice was solid all week. I'm ready to go tomorrow night." He realized he was veering close to begging. But if the Pirates didn't want him, fine. "I don't want the trade."

"I'm doing everything I can, Wes."

"I hate being jerked around."

Victor wasn't only his agent, he was an old family friend. If anyone understood why he didn't want to move again, his life uprooted by the whim of someone in authority, it was Victor.

A seagull had spotted the dog and its paper-bag prize and dived down, beak extended. The dog scampered across the sidewalk, dodging around the feet of pedestrians, veering close to the traffic.

"I have to go," Wes said. He ended the call without waiting for Victor's response and was off the steps in one smooth motion.

"Hey, dog! Stop! Come!" The bird dived again and the dog darted between a lamppost and a bench. "Sit!"

Two women with shopping bags in their hands stared at him.

He spun, scooped his sandwich off the steps and turned back to the street.

There. The dog sprinted between two cars and

slipped past the front wheel of a delivery truck. Just when it appeared to be safely on the opposite sidewalk, it turned to dart back across the street.

The dog was so small.

Wes ripped a hunk off the sandwich and threw it. "Hey, dog, come! Fetch!"

The bird swooped low and the dog skidded past the back wheel of a red car.

He was an idiot. A Spanish dog would know Spanish commands. *How the hell do you say "Heel" in Spanish?* He pulled another piece off his sandwich and held it out as bait while he skirted a trio of twentysomething back-packing tourists and stepped off the sidewalk.

He couldn't see the dog anymore, but a truck loaded with full barrels suddenly accelerated into a gap in the traffic.

The truck's bumper caught him on the hip, his head snapped back into the grille, and then he went flying backward into the outdoor seating at the Savion café. A crack as he landed on one of the café's stone planters told him his barely healed shoulder was done for good.

Hallelujah, he thought right before he passed out from pain.

HE WOKE UP, momentarily disoriented in the dark, but quickly realized he was in a hospital bed. Weak light streaming in from the hall reflected off the machines surrounding him, as an electric hum droned too low to disturb the person slumped in a chair next to his bed. He rubbed his face, surprised to find thick stubble, and

...ered how long he'd been out. His throat was dry ...d he coughed.

The figure in the chair started, sitting up straight and staring at him. *Deacon.* Of course he was here.

"Wes? You're awake?" His brother stood and bent over the bed. He touched Wes's hair and then dropped his hand to rest on his arm. "God, it's good to see you, man."

"What happened to the dog?" Wes asked.

"Dog?"

"Little white one." The details were fuzzy, but he remembered the dog. "It was in the street."

"I don't know anything about a dog." Deacon squinted at him. "You were chasing a dog?"

"It didn't listen. Didn't speak English," Wes clarified. "Was going to get hit by a car."

A deep ache down the left side of his body reminded him that he'd been the one who got hit. There'd been an impact and then that awful crack when he landed. The memory of the cracking sound almost made him pass out again. He moved his arm and felt a throbbing pain under his right shoulder blade. He winced and his older brother's hand tightened on his arm. Deacon's dirty-blond hair was limp and his eyes were shot with red behind his glasses.

"You need a shower," Wes muttered.

Deacon rolled his eyes. "Sorry. I've been distracted. My brother got hit by a beer truck."

Wes shifted again and the pain deepened.

"No more jokes. Laughing hurts." He closed his eyes for a second. "Everything hurts."

"This dog…"

Wes made an effort and opened his eyes.

"You were trying to save it?" Deacon hooked the chair behind him with his foot and pulled it closer so he could sit down, all without moving his hand from Wes's arm. Which was strange. Deacon wasn't the most demonstrative guy and, while he'd been the only real parent Wes ever had, he'd never been the motherly, hovering type. Growing up, Wes had been clipped on the back of the head way more often than he'd had his hand held.

"I didn't want it to get hit."

Deacon pushed his glasses up on his forehead and rubbed his eyes. He readjusted his glasses. "Oh. That's good then." He patted Wes's arm. "A dog ran into the road. That's good."

Why the hell was Deacon *patting* him?

"No, it's not—" His mind finally cleared enough for him to realize what was wrong with his brother. "Why are you here, D.?"

"You got hit by a truck."

"You think I walked in front of it on purpose."

Deacon's denial came a second too late. "No. But Victor did say you were upset…."

Wes groaned and not from pain this time. If he could have moved his right arm without passing out, he'd have punched his brother.

"Upset, yes. They're trading me to Serbia. Fabi is furious. I don't want to move again." Deacon was watching him closely. "I wouldn't kill myself over basketball. Come on."

At that moment Wes realized his brother had been worried precisely because Deacon *could* imagine killing himself over basketball. It was a fundamental difference between them.

Deacon had put every single one of his dreams into his basketball career and when it was cut short by an injury, he'd been lost.

That was when he turned his attention to nurturing Wes's talent for the game. With his brother's support, Wes got to a great college, played on a powerhouse team and, when the NBA passed him over, found this spot on the Madrid team. He'd expected to keep playing ball for at least a few more years, but... The memory of the accident washed back over him and he felt sick to his stomach. The truck hadn't caught him head-on, thank God, but that sound when he hit the ground... He suspected he'd be hearing it in nightmares for the rest of his life.

"How long have I been out?"

"Three days," Deacon said.

"You talked to the doctors?"

Wes gave his brother credit for holding eye contact when he nodded.

He'd never had the passion for the game that Deacon did, but he'd loved playing. Loved being a player, out on the court with the crowd around him. He felt alive when he was the focus of that attention in a way he'd rarely been able to duplicate off the court.

He hadn't wanted to move to Serbia and certainly hadn't thrown himself in front of a truck in despair, but that didn't mean he was ready for the news he was sure was coming next.

Deacon took his glasses off and rubbed his eyes again. "Your shoulder's done. It was touch-and-go the first time. That doctor from the team, Peter? He said you pulled off a miracle after the surgery, working it back into shape. You'll be able to use it. But you're not going to get back to the team."

Wes let his eyes shut again. *You're not going to get back to the team.*

So that was it.

Not going to get back...

He should be wrecked. Run down by a beer truck trying to save a dog, and now unemployed. From living the dream—playing professional basketball, traveling with the team all over Europe, dating gorgeous women—to the end of his career at the age of twenty-eight. For the past twenty years, either he or Deacon had been playing at the top levels of the game. End of an era. The Fallon era.

"You okay?" Wes asked his brother.

"Shouldn't that be my line?"

"Seriously, Deacon."

"Seriously, Wes. You're lying in a hospital bed, your career is over and, judging by the fact that this—" Deacon pointed out an enormous bunch of pink tulips "—is from the truck driver who hit you, while this—" he pointed to a tiny cactus in a black, plastic pot "—is from Fabi, I'm going out on a limb to guess you no longer have a girlfriend." Deacon held up his hand. "Not that I'm bummed about that because Fabi is a…well, you know."

Wes did know. Fabi was living proof you can't judge a book by its cover. She was gorgeous. Long legs, toned muscles, perfect skin, fantastic smile. Underneath the surface was a sketchy moral code and an endless appetite for Wes's money.

He'd loved her brains, though, and her wicked sense of humor. But he hadn't been surprised or heartbroken when she threatened to dump him if he got traded. He'd been more bothered when he realized he wasn't going to fight for the relationship. What had he been doing with her if he wasn't willing to fight for her? The not-so-subtle subtext of the cactus seemed to indicate that being hit by a truck was right up there with being traded to Serbia as a deal breaker.

This breakup fell squarely in the category of not missing things you never really had in the first place.

He wasn't worried about losing Fabi, but Deacon was another question. He couldn't remember a time when he wasn't trying to get Deacon's attention or make him happy. Their mom died when Wes was two. He and Deacon had been split up in foster care until he turned eight and Deacon, a full ten years older, got drafted into the NBA and immediately applied for custody of him. After the guardianship ended when he turned eighteen, Deacon had stayed fully involved in his life.

Mostly through basketball.

Now, for the first time, there was nothing tying him to Deacon. His brother had married his girlfriend, Julia, a little more than seven years ago. They had a full plate running the Fallon Foundation Centers and caring for the teenagers they took in as foster kids.

Without basketball, where would his relationship with Deacon land?

For that matter, what would his life look like? It had emptied out in the seconds after he got hit by that truck.

He could do anything. He'd owed a debt to his brother and he'd fulfilled it by playing as long and as well as he could.

"You want to go back to sleep?" Deacon asked.

"In a minute." He tried to pull the sheet up, but the movement hurt too much. His brother took over, settling it around his shoulders.

"I'm going to get a nurse in here."

Wes hoped the nurse would give him something to take the edge off the pain so he could sleep. "You sure you didn't hear anything about a dog? Not in the accident report or anything?"

Deacon shook his head. "Nothing. I wish someone had told me about it. I wouldn't have been so worried that—" He stood quickly. "Listen, Wes, Julia said I should wait until you're feeling better, but I'm just going to lay this out there. You don't have to say yes or no right away."

Wes really wanted the drugs he was imagining the nurse would bring as soon as Deacon stopped acting out this Lifetime-movie moment.

"Spit it out."

"I have this job and I want you to take it. I want you to come work for me."

"A job?"

"Something to keep you busy."

"I know what a job is. What do you have in mind?"

"You know the Hand-to-Hand pilot program?"

"Yes."

Deacon and Julia ran the Fallon Foundation, building centers offering sports, arts and tutoring programs in economically depressed towns. The Hand-to-Hand program would make sister center relationships between Fallon centers and those in wealthier locations. The program's mission statement said, Everyone needs a hand sometimes and everyone has something to offer.

"We have the site identified—it's a town called Kirkland, right on Kueka Lake. We need the town to give us the lease on the space we've picked out, but it means getting a waiver from them. We're in the last steps of negotiating a partner grant with Robinson University to fund a high-tech tutoring service to three other Fallon centers in New York State. I could really use someone on the ground full-time in Kirkland who can build goodwill and spread the word so we can close both those deals."

Wes's head had started throbbing. Hard work didn't scare him, but he wasn't sure what Deacon was asking him to do, let alone if he'd be capable of doing it.

"Don't you want someone with experience?"

"Weren't you the social chairman of your fraternity?"

"Yes, but you're not asking me to hire a deejay. You want—"

"Shut up and listen. Didn't the Madrid team make you do the press conferences after the games because your sound bites were more entertaining than half the games?"

He needed his brother to shut up so he could get some drugs. "What's your point?"

"My point is, this job is about making people like and want to help the Fallon Foundation. You know our business and people like you."

Wes stared at his brother.

"I don't understand it, either," Deacon said. "But they do."

"Don't you need a marketing guy? I majored in electrical engineering."

"And I would trust you to rewire my toaster." His brother nodded. "I would. I would *also* trust you to show Kirkland exactly what the Fallon Foundation Center is and why they need us in their town. If we get the Hand-to-Hand partnerships going, our ability to bring changes to other communities is going to double. Help me bring that home, Wes."

Since he ultimately owed his life to his brother, when the rare opportunity for him to help came along, he never said no. He had very little understanding of what Deacon wanted him to do, but that was beside the point.

He nodded, which sent the throbbing inside his head off the charts.

Deacon's jaw tightened. He leaned forward as if he

was going to pat Wes again or maybe hug him, but he said simply, "I'll get the nurse."

A few minutes later, with what felt like a very effective painkiller finally pumping through his IV, Wes started drifting off again. Deacon was on the phone, talking softly.

"He's going to do it, Julia. I know you wanted me to wait, but I needed to get him settled." A pause. "He said there was a dog in the street. He was trying to grab it."

Wes closed his eyes.

Deacon's voice was almost a whisper. Wes might have missed what he said next, but he didn't.

"How do I know if it's the truth? I want it to be. He's not going to tell me and you know it. We'll keep an eye on him. What else can we do?"

IT WAS ANOTHER THREE DAYS before the doctors were satisfied that he was recovered enough to discharge him. Wes didn't tell Deacon he'd overheard him. He noticed that his brother was never out of the room long, and twice he woke up to find Deacon staring at him.

The constant scrutiny was disconcerting. Did Deacon really think he'd have tried to kill himself over the Serbia trade?

When he was awake, they went over the Hand-to-Hand center in painstaking detail. By the time he was ready to leave the hospital, Wes was pretty sure he knew more about Kirkland, N.Y., than the mayor of the town. (Jay Meacham, age forty-six. Kirkland High, class of

1980, guard on the lunchtime basketball team at the Y, scotch and soda, never married.)

In the span of a week, he'd been hit by a truck, released by his team and educated in the history and traditions of one very small town in New York in preparation for the new job he hadn't applied for and didn't really know how to do. Life was dragging him along again. And he felt just as impotent now as he had when he'd heard about the trade to Serbia. The situation was different, because he was helping Deacon, but somehow it felt the same.

He went back to the apartment he'd been sharing with two of his teammates and took three days to pack up his life and say his goodbyes. On the streets, he kept an eye out for the little dog, but it never showed up. On the upside, his roommates swore they hadn't seen it dead by the side of the road, either. Maybe it had found a new home.

At the next home game, Wes's last, the arena was packed. Wes gave a farewell speech at halftime and as he ran through the joking acknowledgments he'd written for his teammates, he looked into the stands. Was this it? The final time he'd be at center court, entertaining a crowd?

That night he made the very bad decision to go out for a tour of nightclubs with the team. He ran into Fabi, who made a big deal over his scar and then tried to drag him into a private room to make out. He thanked her for the cactus and declined the invitation.

When he woke up the next morning he quickly dis-

covered his teammates had given him a thoughtful part-
ing gift. His usual thick hair was gone, shorn down to
patchy stubble.

He was staring at himself in the bathroom mirror and
wondering if he had time to hunt down Gary Krota to
make him eat his razor, when his brother called.

"We have a problem," Deacon said. "This woman in
Kirkland, Trish Jones, ran a fundraiser for us last month.
All her own idea and effort, but she used our name and
logo. I didn't actually know about it until she'd been pro-
moting the event for a few days and by then it was too
late to cut her off. She got the community involved and
we had to be careful because we need as much goodwill as we can muster."

Wes turned away from his reflection and leaned back
on the sink.

"What'd she do, organize a bake sale? It's not warm
enough for a car wash there, is it?"

"She wrote a blog post and put up a donation button.
The Kirkland paper said she managed to rake in over
sixty-five thousand dollars. In ten days."

Wes whistled. "That's not true."

"Honest to God. She told them she wasn't expecting
that kind of number, but apparently some other local
blogger with a much bigger audience got wind of the
thing and shared the link to Trish's fundraising site and
it snowballed."

"Seventy thousand dollars?"

"It's going to buy a lot of basketballs. Except there's
a little problem."

"It's all in pennies?"

"Trish hasn't answered her phone in the past week."

"You think she skipped town?"

"She owns a business there," Deacon said. "I want to believe there's an innocent explanation, but the other blogger, Chloe Chastain, called us with her concerns. Her reputation is on the line, too. When you get to Kirkland tomorrow, Trish Jones is your number one priority. We need to know where that money is and we need it to be in our bank account, safe and accounted for as soon as possible."

"Got it." Wes turned back to the mirror. Gary Krota better hope he never had to make a living as a barber.

POSY JONES SPENT one weekend, every other month, in her mother's house in Kirkland, New York.

Trish cared what the other women on the Kirkland mom-and-community circuit thought about her and while Posy was often frustrated by her mom, she loved her. So she showed up and did her time and her mom had stories to tell her friends to prove that her relationship with her daughter was just as nice and perfect as she wanted it to be.

Timing the visits also capped the amount of crazy she had to deal with. Her mom had a habit of stepping into trouble and expecting Posy to bail her out, and the problems tended to snowball if she was away from Kirkland too long.

She flicked the button on the steering wheel to turn off the radio, silencing the Kirkland morning show—

the same deejay team that had woken Posy up every morning in junior high school.

Before she got out of the car, she turned her phone on. Not a single missed call from her mom during the three-hour trip from Rochester. *That* never happened. She'd only spoken to her mom briefly the day before, too. When was the last time her mom had kept her on the phone longer than two minutes? Last week?

Main Street in downtown Kirkland was picturesque. As a location scout and quality control inspector for a national hotel chain, Posy was a professional at assessing the up- and downsides to communities. Kirkland was almost all upside—small, but thriving downtown full of locally owned businesses, excellent public schools, a pretty setting tucked on the shore of one of the Finger Lakes in upstate New York.

The downtown streets were lined with hanging baskets of flowers. Recycled plastic benches were spaced at friendly intervals to encourage visiting and lingering. A decent run of tourists came through in the summer for wine tours and lake camping. Another run in the fall for the foliage. Robinson University was a steady employer, and brought outlets for culture, a decent roster of small, research spin-off companies, as well as a solid but ever-changing population to fill rental units. And that bolstered the bottom line of countless Kirkland family budgets.

If she were assessing her hometown as a possible site for one of the Hotel Marie's locations, she'd have to give Kirkland excellent marks. The year-round population was too small to support a large hotel like those in her chain, but she wouldn't be able to fault much else.

That, however, was only the professional assessment. Personally? Posy gave Kirkland a lot more X marks than checks.

Posy's parents separated when she was nine. Her dad moved to Rochester and her mom used every trick she could think of to drag the separation out and avoid divorce. When the divorce was finally official, Posy was fifteen and the family court judge allowed her to choose the custodial parent. She picked her dad, which precipitated an immediate campaign of guilt-tripping and pity parties from her mom. That campaign was still going strong thirteen years later.

As Trish never failed to mention, her dad hadn't been willing or able to give Posy the kind of attention she'd been used to receiving from her mom. Which had been the point of Posy's choice, but Trish would never accept that. It was a true story, but not a pretty one. And Trish would pick fantasy over harsh reality every time.

She found a parking place a few doors down from the Wonders of Christmas Shoppe, the store her mom owned on Main Street. Usually when she visited she did everything in her power to avoid Wonders, but her mom had insisted they meet there. She parked and locked her car, a habit she'd picked up when she moved to Rochester with her dad and that marked her as an outsider in Kirkland. Appropriate, because she'd never really fit in here in the first place.

The day was warm and there was a short line waiting for an outdoor table at the Lemon Drop Café. Wonders, on the other hand, had a Closed sign on the front door and the white lights that twinkled around the window display year-round were off. The brass door handle didn't turn when she tried it. Posy knocked on the glass. She saw movement in the back of the store and waited while her mom made her way from the office.

Trish Jones turned the lock and pulled the door open with a jingle of brass bells. Posy was caught in a cinnamon-scented hug, gently patting her mom's back while trying to ignore the familiar awkwardness she felt whenever they touched. Posy was six feet tall, more than ten inches taller than Trish. Her frame was built on a completely different scale, broad and sturdy, quick to add muscle versus will-o'-the-wisp insubstantial. It was a size difference that, when Posy shot up past her mom early in fifth grade, had only exacerbated their constant conflicts over what Trish termed Posy's unwillingness to fit in. She'd somehow managed to believe that Posy had willed herself into being a freakishly tall girl in middle school. Because that was exactly the fate every eleven-year-old girl longed for.

"I'm so glad you're finally here, sweetheart," Trish said. "I missed you."

She released Posy, opened the door and quickly glanced up and down the street before closing and locking it again. Posy braced herself to be told that her orange T-shirt was too bright or that her freshly painted nails in their deep eggplant glory were disturbing.

"Did you see anyone out there? Chloe?"

"Anyone besides all the people walking around town on a gorgeous spring afternoon? No." Posy squinted toward the Lemon Drop. "Chloe Chastain?"

"Never mind," her mom said. "I'm glad you're here."

Two "glad you're heres" in one minute? No critique of her outfit?

"Come back to the office," Trish said.

Posy's large leather purse held her iPad, iPhone, travel mug, business cards, emergency travel kit, makeup kit and was basically her life. Rather than risk maneuvering through the store with it on her shoulder, she set it on the tile near the front door.

She was about to follow her mom toward the back of the store when she heard a soft thump behind her.

Her mom's tiny, white schnoodle, Angel, had jumped from the raised window display and now crouched on the floor near the bag. With fluffy white fur, round black eyes and a perky green plaid bow on her red leather collar, Angel looked the part of the perfect Christmas-shop accessory dog.

She eyed Angel. The dog's tail twitched—a silent-movie villain's mustache twirl.

Nonchalantly, Posy stretched one hand toward the bag, but she was too slow. With another quick swish of her tail, the dog shoved her face into Posy's bag and emerged with her acid-yellow, leather business card wallet clutched between small, white teeth.

"No. Angel, drop it!"

Angel disappeared under the skirt around the table holding a model-train display with a village skating rink as the centerpiece. The tiny bell in the steeple of the chapel jingled when the dog bumped against the table leg. Posy knew from unfortunate experience that there'd be no catching Angel, and less than no chance the dog would do something as helpful as obey a command. She didn't even bother lifting the table skirt. If Angel had a Twitter account and opposable thumbs, she'd send the #SillyHumans hash tag trending every day.

"Angel is under stress right now," Trish said. Which was a new one. Sometimes Angel was delicate. Other times she'd eaten something that didn't agree with her. The one true explanation for her dog's terrible behavior—that Angel was a demon-spawned obedience-school dropout in a fluffy white fur coat—was never mentioned. "I'll replace that…whatever it was."

Posy lifted her bag, looking in vain for a spare inch or two on one of the tables where she could put it out of the dog's reach. She ended up slinging it over her shoulder, holding it tight against her side with one arm.

Her mom bustled toward the back of the store. "I'm unpacking a shipment. Come on and I can tell you the news," she said. "Watch that garland!"

Posy stooped to duck under a rope of gold, spray-painted eucalyptus leaves and pinecones. She turned sideways to edge past a display of the beautifully detailed, handcrafted papier-mâché mangers her mom commissioned from an artist in Pennsylvania.

Wonders didn't have aisles so much as narrow alleys between displays crammed full of Christmas glitz and glitter. From the handblown ornaments hanging on color-coordinated trees, to the loops of beaded crystal garland Posy ducked through as she passed the register, the store carried everything and anything Christmas and delicate.

Her mom's real specialty was miniatures. Wonders was the best-stocked retail outlet on the East Coast for holiday decorators who took verisimilitude in their train displays or light-up Christmas villages to the extreme. Every inch of horizontal space inside Wonders contained tiny, detailed, uncannily realistic miniatures and scene scapes.

Posy ran a hand over the thick nap of an ivory, velvet tree skirt. She'd worn more than her fair share of velvet Christmas dresses when she was in elementary school. Each one had been beautiful on the hanger, but the heavy fabric and childish styles had exaggerated Posy's large frame, making her feel even more self-conscious. Trish had exquisite sewing skills—she just didn't have any gauge to tell her when enough was so much more than enough.

In the crowded back office, her mom was bent over an open cardboard box, Bubble Wrap mounded around her ankles. A ceramic angel lay on the carpet next to her feet. She didn't look up as Posy came in, but said, "See that envelope on my desk?"

Posy nodded and then realized her mom, who was unwrapping another angel, couldn't see her. "Yes."

"It's for you. Open it up."

The envelope was blank, no return address or mailing labels, and Posy couldn't help feeling curious as she undid the metal clasp and slid the sheaf of stapled pages out.

She read the first few lines of the top sheet, then quickly leafed through the attached deeds and mortgage documents. "Mom?"

Trish put the second angel down and then lowered herself to her knees to reach deep into the box in front of her. "It's your legacy, Posy."

The papers listed all her mom's assets, the house, Wonders, a two-year-old minivan and a safe-deposit box at the bank.

"My what?"

"Your legacy. From me to you."

Her mom was trying to give her all the clutter Posy had been doing her best to keep strictly out of her own life for the past twenty years.

Posy was both touched and horrified. "This isn't a legacy, it's—" *An albatross.* "Mom…"

"Posy. You've been telling me for years that I need to sell the house, haven't you? It's too big for one person. And every time I add a new product line to the store, you accuse me of slipping one step closer to a hoarding diagnosis."

Posy nodded. She felt completely confused and a finger of panic crept up her back. Surely her mom wasn't planning to leave Kirkland. Where would she go? *Rochester?* Posy's brand-new condo?

"Well, consider your advice taken. I'm selling everything. To you."

"Selling?" Posy said, looking more closely at the

pages. "Oh, Mom, it's a nice impulse, but I just bought my condo. I don't need your house or your car, and I can't take care of Wonders. And where are you going to live? What's going on?" She paused as fear crept into her gut, making her queasy. "Wait, why are you doing this? Are you okay? Everything's okay, right?"

Posy set the legal papers aside and took a good look at her mom. Friends often described Trish as animated. Her ash-blond hair and bright green eyes were different enough from Posy's black hair and dark brown eyes that they'd never be mistaken for relatives, let alone mother and daughter. Even though her mom was pretty, as sparkling as one of her ornaments, Posy noticed now that there was something different about Trish. Was the sparkle only a fever?

"I'm in love." Trish clasped her hands over her heart. Actually clasped them and closed her eyes. She was a Precious Moments statue come to life.

Her mom spent *way* too much time looking at snow globe scenes.

CHAPTER TWO

"You're in love?" Posy stared at her mom, who was still clasping her hands to her heart. Still surrounded by Bubble Wrap.

"Mitch. His name is Mitch. He's a bit older than me. He was a surgeon—worked on hands—and he's retired now out in Ohio, with pots of money. We've been corresponding online since last October, and seeing each other for three months. Posy, you won't believe this, but he loves me. He loves everything about me and he wants me to move in with him."

Trish was right. Posy didn't quite believe it. After her marriage broke up, Trish had become increasingly needy and clingy when anyone so much as asked her on a date.

Posy had a clear memory of a guy who'd come to pick Trish up for a first date being coerced into fixing the washing machine. He hadn't come back for a second date. For Trish, love meant never having to solve your own problems. Not too many men stuck around after the first crisis.

It had been several years since her mom had gone out with anyone, as far as Posy knew. Despite her daily phone calls and innumerable weekly texts, she'd been keeping this guy a secret for three months?

"A surgeon? Where did you meet?"

If her mom said Match.com, she was going straight to the FBI to get a profile of this supposed surgeon/paragon. She felt disloyal, but it was hard to believe Trish had met a guy and hadn't scared him off. That had never happened, in all of Posy's twenty-eight years.

"We met at the Holiday World trade show. I was testing a line of nutcrackers, which if anyone ever tries to tell you resin composites look exactly like hand-carved wood, you should run the other way. But anyway, Mitch noticed that I was uncomfortable with the salesman's hard sell and he stepped in and put a stop to it."

Anyone who helped her mom walk away from an investment in faux-wood, resin-composite nutcrackers won bonus points in Posy's book.

"Why was he looking at nutcrackers?"

"He wasn't. He was buying antique-style streetlights for his train display. The wires are so thin you can barely see them. I'll show you—"

"Mom! The surgeon."

"He's retired. He owns a wonderful place near Toledo called Mitch's Train Yard. It's this incredible Christmas train display that fills his whole barn. He has a shop and a small café and is building up a model-train museum."

"Your new boyfriend is a model-train-collecting professional?" Was there any way this was true? Had her mom actually met a guy who would not only put up with her crazy collections, but enjoy them? Share them? *Contribute to them?*

"We're perfect for each other. It's too bad your dad isn't still here. I think he'd have enjoyed meeting Mitch."

Posy's dad would have hanged himself with a string of Christmas lights before he got anywhere near a meeting with her mom's new boyfriend. But she didn't say that to her mother. In the three years since he'd died, Trish had been mentally revising their relationship until it would be hard to know from her stories that after their divorce Posy's dad had gone out of his way to avoid her company.

Trish became absorbed again in the angels. She picked one up and ran a finger over the gilded wings. "So once you write me a check, I'll be free and clear and I can move in with him."

"Mom, I'm not buying all your stuff so you can run away to Toledo. Don't get me wrong, I'm happy for you." And happy that her mom was finally willing to consider downsizing. The house and store were the sources of many of the problems Posy had been called in to manage, but as much as she wanted them gone, she didn't want her mom rushing into a relationship with a virtual stranger. "You don't have to move right away. What if we make a plan—we'll talk to a Realtor, get someone to look at the accounts for the store and see if you can attract a buyer. Even if you just want to liquidate the stock, you need to think this through."

Trish was shaking her head.

"No? What no? Mom, is there something else you're keeping from me?"

"I don't want to get into the details." Trish's hands tightened on the angel and she broke the left-hand wing off. "Oh, no." Her shoulders hunched up close to her ears and she seemed to shrink right in front of Posy. "I'd rather not discuss it."

If Posy hadn't already guessed there was something very wrong going on in her mom's life, that would have been an unavoidable clue. If Trish didn't want to discuss something, it was Upsetting or Uncomfortable or even worse, Embarrassing. She'd happily chat about cancer, crime, war, politics, heck, even religion, but as soon as the conversation brushed up against shame or negative image, Trish shut the door.

"Mom, you didn't really think I was going to buy every one of your earthly possessions without finding out why this is necessary."

"I told you the reason. Mitch. He's a hand surgeon. I'm going to move to Ohio."

Patented Trish Jones "looking on the bright side" nonsense.

"Bullshit."

Trish pressed her hands together and her mouth tightened briefly before she smoothed her expression. "Posy, there's no need for that type of language."

"Tell me why you need money all of a sudden. Is this guy pulling some kind of scam?"

"No!" Trish practically shouted. "He doesn't know. The truth is… I'm not sure how to… I need the money because…" Trish sniffed and shook her head as she picked up the pieces of the broken angel and tried to fit them back together, but she only managed to chip the end off the wing. Angel, the dog, zipped in out of nowhere and scooped the piece of ceramic off the floor before running back out into the store. "Because I don't want to go to jail."

Of all the things that had come out of her mother's mouth over the years, that had to be about the most shocking. *Jail?* Trish Jones? Cardigan-sweater wearer, volunteer for good causes, poodle aficionado, owner of a Christmas shop spelled with an extra *P* and an *E*?

"*Jail?*"

The wing snapped off a second angel her mom had picked up.

"Put the angels down before you massacre the whole heavenly host, okay?"

"I didn't want to tell you this," Trish said. "It would have been so much easier if you'd bought everything. I could have paid the money back and no one would ever have known."

"What money?"

"I ran a fundraiser. It was just a small thing. I put a story on my Wonders blog about the community center we're trying to open here. Some of my readers wanted to help, so I set up a donation button. But then Chloe Chastain linked to it from her blog and her readership is much larger than mine—mommy bloggers have a big reach. Before I knew it, I'd collected quite a bit of money."

Posy was having trouble tracking the details. She read her mom's blog, but she had a very small core of regular commenters, fellow Christmas-shop owners and miniatures enthusiasts. Chloe—her old neighbor—ran a blog that was a different story. She'd somehow turned a twice-daily post about life as a divorced mom, taking her toddlers to the park or sipping wine from a plastic Barbie cup, into a successful business. Posy didn't *read* Chloe's blog, but she did look at it from time to time. She had to do *something* while waiting for movies to load on Netflix.

"Mom, the crime?"

"I don't have the money anymore."

She doesn't have the money anymore. Oh, Lord.

Posy coaxed the details out of her. Trish had been shocked at the amount of money people donated. She'd told a friend of hers about it and the friend had asked to borrow the money. Trish's friend ran a Christmas store in Maine and her credit line had been reduced by her bank. She told Trish she just needed the money for a few days while she collected on several overdue accounts.

Posy's voice shook as she asked, "When is she going to pay you back?"

"I'm afraid I was taken in. She lied about her situation, Posy. She declared bankruptcy last week and her assets are frozen. I'm not going to get the money back."

"I don't understand why you lent it to her in the first place."

"She sounded like she really needed the help. This

economy has been so hard for so many of my friends. I couldn't say no when she needed help."

Which was close to the truth, but not exactly the whole truth. Trish needed to be loved. She collected emotional debts the same way she collected miniatures—fervently and to an extreme. If her friend told her she would be eternally grateful for the loan, Trish would have had a hard time turning her down.

"Now Chloe Chastain keeps calling me. She wants to know when the Fallon Foundation is going to acknowledge the gift. She says she's accountable to her blog readers. Posy, she's going to tell everyone what I did."

Everyone including the police.

"So that's where I come in? I buy your stuff so you can pay the money back without anyone finding out?"

Trish nodded.

They needed a list. Figure out how much her mom owed and then sell whatever they had to or even get a loan to pay it off. Glancing around the office for a piece of paper and a pen, she realized she was still holding the deeds to her legacy. Wonders, the house. Trish's car. Her safe-deposit box where she kept her grandmother's diamond earrings. Did her mom really think she could write a check to cover all that?

Oh, no.

"Mom, how much money did you collect?"

"Sixty-eight thousand dollars. Sixty-eight thousand, eight hundred and seventy-six dollars, actually."

Posy leaned against the desk and fanned herself with the papers. She wondered if she was going to vomit.

"Sixty-eight—" she was barely able to form the words "—thousand dollars? From your blog?"

"Chloe's blog gets twenty thousand hits a day."

"Sixty-eight thousand dollars?" She couldn't stop repeating the number. It seemed absurd, but Trish kept nodding in confirmation. She'd thought they were dealing with a few thousand, ten at the most. How in the heck had she raised that much money?

How big was Chloe's audience, anyway?

When she'd recovered enough to ask questions, the answers she got were even more alarming. Trish was in serious debt. Wonders had limped along for several years, never straying too far into the red or the black. She'd sold the building a few years ago when it needed a new roof and an upgraded fire-suppression system, and she couldn't afford to bring it up to code. After the economy went downhill, Trish mortgaged her house twice to keep Wonders going. The final blow came when she'd mismanaged the holiday ordering the previous Christmas. Now Wonders was about as sunk as a shoppe could get without actually closing its doors.

She'd gone to her bank in a panic this week to try to get a loan to pay the fundraiser back, but she had no assets and bad credit and she'd been turned down flat.

Of all the dramas her mother had created over the years, this one was far and away the most insane. Posy was accustomed to bailing her mom out of jams and patching up messes.... She'd held her hand through an IRS audit a few years ago. This was unbelievable, though.

It had to stop. Trish's cycle of crisis and collapse was too much. Posy had lost too much time, skipped too many dates, changed too many plans over the years.

Covering up a crime, even if it was only a temporary crime, was the last straw. If she was ever going to have her own life, Posy thought, she needed to… She had trouble finishing that thought. She couldn't cut her mom out of her life. She just needed her mom to stop screwing up.

"Posy, this is all so complicated. How am I going to get out from under my obligations here so I can go to Ohio?"

Ohio? Trish was worried about not being able to move to Toledo? Posy didn't want to upset her, but she really needed to be thinking about how to stay out of jail.

"If only you hadn't broken things off with Pete. You'd probably be married by now and he was very good with math."

"Pete would not have helped you with this. He'd have been paralyzed with fear about possible police involvement."

She and her last boyfriend had been together for three years and although Trish had her hopes set on an engagement, Posy had realized that what she'd initially liked about Pete—his deference to her and willingness to compromise—drove her nuts. He was like a puppy, constantly rolling on his back to expose his vulnerable belly. By the time she ended things with him, she'd been eyeing that belly with the urge to give him a swift kick. She hadn't liked herself very much by that point.

"We need time and we need money. Chloe is a problem, but we'll figure out a way to put her off. What about the foundation? The one you raised the money for? Are they suspicious?"

"There's a man—"

"A man?"

CHAPTER THREE

"WHAT MAN?"

"A man from the foundation. He'll be here tomorrow to meet me and Chloe and collect his check." Trish practically whispered the last few words.

When she said the word *check,* Trish put her hands over her mouth as if she could hold back the terror Posy heard in her voice.

She crossed the room to kneel next to her mom. It was a tight fit and she banged her ankle on the leg of the desk. She angled her arms around her mom's shoulders. The cinnamon scent from the sachets her mother kept in her drawers was strong and familiar.

"I don't have that kind of money saved, Mom. Buying my condo took almost all my cash. I'd lend it to you if I could. We'll figure this out. I'll help. Whatever I can do, I'm here for you."

For a second, her mom seemed to cling to her, but then she abruptly straightened up.

"Well, I guess it's on to plan B."

"We have a plan B?"

Trish stood and brushed the front of her skirt. She stepped out of the jumble of packing materials, the two angels lying broken on the floor.

"Of course I have a plan B. My aunt Denise will lend me the money. She's always been very generous and she didn't blink an eye when I asked her for a loan."

"You already asked her?" Posy was lost again.

"Yes, but I wanted to give you the chance to inherit first. I'm going to drive down to the city and see her. You stay here and stall the Fallon Foundation man and Chloe. I'll be back in a few days with the money and everything will be fine."

Posy knew that tone. Her mom was looking on the bright side again. "You really called Aunt Denise? Why not just have her send the check?"

"Posy, I'm borrowing close to seventy-thousand dollars from a lonely old woman who's always been very kind to me. The least I can do is stop in for an afternoon chat."

Bam. Her mother was the queen at making you feel stupid while also getting her own way. She didn't like this, but what was she going to do? "I'll keep the foundation people and Chloe at bay, but this has to be the last time."

"What do you mean?"

"I mean, if we sell your house and close down Wonders, then your life is your own. You can spend time with your new guy or stay in Kirkland, but you have to promise me you're going to get yourself together. I need to have my independence."

Trish kissed her cheek. "I promise."

Posy nodded. "Then I'm in."

THAT NIGHT AFTER she was sure her mom was asleep, Posy slid out of bed in the guest room. Her mom had never redecorated her childhood bedroom and the pink-and-white color scheme and fussy flounces attached to every surface from the curtains to the comforter to the skirt on the vanity table made her claustrophobic.

She didn't turn the light on as she walked down the carpeted upstairs hall and then quietly continued down the sweeping staircase to the foyer. Her mom and dad bought the house when the development it was in had still been a blueprint in the model house's showcase living room. Trish picked out all the fixtures and upgrades and she'd clung stubbornly to the house even after her husband moved out.

If Trish had been able to admit back then that her life would never be the picture-perfect image she'd wanted, would she be in the same mess today? If she had dealt with the hole her divorce left in her life, would she have been so desperate to connect with other people? Would Posy still be trying to work off the guilt she felt over being the wrong sort of daughter and picking the wrong parent?

That kind of what-if was absurd, especially because her mom was going to finally sell the house. Trish had, thankfully, set up a retirement fund and while she'd recently taken a loan from it, the bulk of her savings was intact. That meant Posy could meet with a Realtor about the house. And when Trish came back, the two of them would talk to an accountant about Wonders.

The house needed a lot of work before it could be

sold. After Posy and her dad moved out, Trish filled up
the empty hours with *stuff.*

Like the display space at Wonders, every corner was
packed with collections and collectibles—everything
from lighthouses, to thimbles to dollhouse furniture.
If only she'd collected something valuable—Matisses,
maybe, or original O'Keeffes. Posy might joke with her
about hoarding, but the truth was, they weren't going to
be able to show the house until they cleared it out. It was
impossible to see the generous space in its current state.

She turned down the hallway, heading for the kitchen,
where she flipped the light on, surprising Angel, who
was crouched near the sliding glass doors staring out
into the dark backyard. The dog jumped and then sat
down with her tail to the doors, watching Posy. If Angel
had been a human, Posy would have thought she was
embarrassed.

"You peeping that golden retriever next door?" Angel
didn't move. "Don't bother. He told me he only likes
smooth-coated chicks. Your curls are a turnoff."

The dog didn't take her eyes off her.

"You've met this Mitch guy? Is he the real deal?"

Angel flopped on the floor, her head resting on
crossed front paws. She lifted the corner of her top lip
in what might have been a yawn, but was more likely
a growl.

Posy sat in one of the black wooden chairs at the
kitchen island. She turned on her iPad and looked up
Mitch's Train Yard. The ex-surgeon looked friendly and
normal in his photo. She'd waited her entire life for

her mom to turn her laser focus and need for love on someone else. Knowing she had a boyfriend explained the relatively few phone calls and texts she'd been getting recently.

She just hoped he was on the up-and-up.

Before she continued her research, Posy called her cousin Maddy.

"The Knoll Retreat and Healing Center. This is Sister Maddy."

"Maddy, it's Posy."

"What's up? I thought you were on your pilgrimage to Trish's house." Maddy's voice was warm and rich, hinting at the singing talent that had sent her to college for musical theater before she switched gears her senior year and pursued a position in the Daughters of Respite religious order. "How are you?"

"I'm at my mom's. I guess I'm going to be here for a couple days, helping out. She's closing Wonders. And selling her house. She met a new guy."

"When did this happen? Didn't I talk to you yesterday?"

"It was fast. Did you know about the fundraiser she hosted last month?"

"Someone forwarded the link. I think the retreat center sent a donation."

As she talked, Posy looked up Chloe Chastain's *It's a Mad, Mad Mommy* blog.

"I'm looking at Chloe Chastain's blog post about it right now. You wouldn't believe how many comments and link backs there are."

"Let me open it up," Maddy said, and Posy listened as her cousin hit some keys. "Whoa. She looks good in that picture."

Mixed in with the fundraising posts were Chloe's regular stock-in-trade photos of her adorable daughters doing adorable things, accompanied by entries written by Chloe, who looked fairly adorable herself at the ripe old age of twenty-six.

"Chloe Chastain always looks good. Bed head is probably afraid of her."

"It figures she'd have a blog about making life perfect. Remember when we were little and she was constantly making us do pretend weddings?" Maddy said. "You'd get so incensed because she made you be the groom."

"I would have been happy being the priest. She just liked to make me mad."

Maddy laughed. "It wasn't as if she had to try very hard. Two people as competitive as you guys are—the conflict was inevitable."

Except for her divorce, it sounded as if Chloe Chastain's life had continued along the small-town-princess line it had been on when they were kids. Trish's most common cause for complaint was that Posy wasn't more like Chloe. There'd been a time when Posy would have sold her soul to be like her neighbor. In Posy's worst memories, Chloe was always there, petite, poised, smart, graceful and so unrelentingly judgmental. Posy never felt more out of step than she did around Chloe.

"Look at the list of people who donated. Most of them aren't even from here," Maddy said. "This is huge."

"My mom stole the money." Posy was whispering even though no one else was around.

There was silence over the line.

Quickly, Posy went on, explaining how her mom had gotten into trouble. "Now this guy from the foundation is coming and I have to hold him off until my mom gets a loan from my aunt."

"Oh. My. Goodness."

"I hope the sisters don't have your phone bugged."

"Posy," her cousin admonished. "Even if the sisters did listen in, they don't have anything to do with punishing people for their sins. We have God for that."

"Thank you, Maddy. You're so kind. I can see why you went into the convent."

"Does Chloe know?"

"No!"

"Because she won't blink at the opportunity to bring your mom down. Imagine the traffic she'd get to her blog with that story? Especially if she can make herself look good in the process. Your mom will be crucified."

Posy didn't answer. What could she say?

"Sorry," Maddy said. "That wasn't helpful."

"You haven't met the guy from the Fallon Foundation when he's been in town, have you?"

"Deacon? He seems very nice."

"His brother, Wes."

"I haven't met that one." She heard Maddy's keyboard. "Let's see what Google says."

Posy knew enough about the world to know that if you were working for a foundation and you had the same last name as the guy who'd endowed it, you were probably privileged.

She typed his name in, too. *Wes.* Who named their kid Wes? People who wanted their kid to get beaten up in elementary school, that was who. His parents had made a bad call on that one.

Maddy's keyboard fell silent and Posy stared at her own screen. Her cousin whistled.

"Your mom stole money from a really good-looking guy."

There were hundreds of pictures of Wes Fallon, alone. The one that made her look twice was from some kind of formal event and showed a clear shot of his face.

The woman with him was wearing a dress slit up past where her underwear should have started. Her hair was tousled so one thick wave fell over her eye. She was undeniably sexy…and trying really, really hard. Wes had his arm around her waist and he was smiling down at her as if he knew she was being foolish, but he was having too much fun to care. Just a ridiculously handsome guy enjoying himself.

She'd always been a sucker for people who knew how to fit in and have fun.

"Call me tomorrow after you meet him, okay?" Maddy said. "And let me know if I can help."

Posy hung up, browsed a few more pages of Wes Fallon pictures and then closed the tab. Now that she'd thoroughly depressed herself, she opened her email to send a message to Wyatt, her boss, that she needed to take some time off. An emergency. She rarely used her vacation, so she knew it wouldn't be a problem. She'd call in tomorrow and talk to him just to be sure.

Four days tops. That was how long they'd estimated it might take for Trish to get to the city, get her aunt's bank to set up a wire transfer and see the money cleared into her account.

If Posy could keep Wes Fallon and Chloe Chastain in the dark about the crime for four days at the most, her mom would be home free. And then maybe if she got rid of all this stuff and set her mom up with the model-train enthusiast, she could finally put down her load of guilt. The one she'd been carrying ever since the family court judge made the final custody arrangements by looking Posy in the eye and saying, "Pick."

WHEN SHE GOT downstairs the next morning, she found a note written on thick white stationery with a red-and-green border and the Wonders logo at the top. Her mom had decided to strike out early for the city to get the money as soon as possible. Posy would meet the man from the foundation at one o'clock. Trish would be in touch as soon as she'd spoken with her aunt.

Posy didn't like this. She and Trish had planned to have breakfast at the Lemon Drop together this morning. Her mom loved to be seen out with her daughter. Why would she skip that and why would she leave a note instead of waking Posy?

She called her mom's cell, but it went straight to voice mail.

She glanced at the note again.

There was a P.S. on the back. Angel's lamb and rice–formula dog food was in a plastic container in the pantry. The best-before date was coming up and Angel had a delicate stomach. If Posy needed to restock, she should be sure to buy the premium food.

Angel lifted her front paw and scratched at the glass sliding door. She wanted out.

"That makes two of us, sugar."

WES BALANCED THE BOX of Hand-to-Hand promotional T-shirts and bumper stickers on his hip as he unlocked the door to his temporary office. He left the key in the lock momentarily while he scratched his head. The hospital staff had had to shave a strip above his ear to stitch up a cut the doctors were pretty sure came from one of the metal parts on the truck's grille. And then, of course, Gary Krota shaved the rest of the hair off on their last night out. The hair growing in not only itched incessantly, it made it impossible for him to forget the accident for longer than five minutes at a time.

Deacon had arranged for him to rent office space in the Kirkland town center. He thought it was a good idea for Wes to be in proximity to the mayor and the members of the town board, who had offices in the building. Without their zoning variance, the site Deacon had picked out wouldn't be approved.

The door swung open when he turned the key, and

Wes stepped inside. The room was cramped, but the two windows set in the back wall made up for the small size. He put the box of shirts and stickers on the floor near the door and let his duffel bag slide to the ground as he opened the blinds. The office overlooked a small staff parking lot and an empty playground behind the building. Midday on a Tuesday didn't seem like a popular time—all the swings were empty and not one kid was on the basketball court.

It was a shame to see such a nice court going to waste.

He hadn't played since his accident, but his doctor had cleared him for normal activities before he left Madrid. His shoulder would need some physical therapy, but it didn't hurt anymore.

He had the ball in his bag.

Flipping the cord, he let the blinds fall back down. *Later.* He was here to do a job for Deacon.

Trish Jones, the lady who collected the donations, was due in just a few minutes. He kicked the duffel bag behind the desk and then opened the box of shirts. Deacon's wife, Julia, said he needed some props for his charm offensive. He was supposed to give the Hand-to-Hand shirts out so that eventually it would seem inevitable to the town that the partnership was going to go through.

Wes left his office and went in search of the Kirkland mayor. He found an office with the mayor's nameplate on the wall. When he knocked on the doorjamb, the young guy sitting behind the desk looked up.

"I'm Wes Fallon, from the Fallon Foundation. I thought I'd say hello to Mayor Meacham."

"Nice to meet you, Mr. Fallon. I've been hoping to meet you." The guy hopped up and came around to shake hands. "Ryan O'Malley, the mayor's special assistant."

"Good to meet you, too," Wes said. Ryan looked as if he'd only recently graduated from college, but he had a firm handshake and his dark suit made Wes wonder if he'd underdressed in dark jeans and a golf shirt.

"The mayor isn't in at the moment, I expect him back shortly," Ryan said. "But I wanted to tell you how much respect I have for the work you're doing. This Hand-to-Hand center is the kind of innovation we need in the community services world."

Wes smiled. "We just have to get the variance and then we'll be all set. In the meantime, can I give you a T-shirt or a sticker?"

Ryan smiled and took one of each. Then he asked for a second shirt for his fiancée.

Wes handed them over, happy to have recruited his first ally in Kirkland.

A short guy with blond hair thinning on the top entered the office. "Hey, there you are, Wes," he said. "Great to see you again."

Wes smiled and nodded even though he didn't know how the guy knew him.

At that moment a tall woman with dark hair glanced into the office, but kept walking down the hall.

"Wes," Ryan said, "this is Mayor Meacham."

"Jay," the mayor said. "Call me Jay." He took Wes's hand and pumped it. "It's good to have you here. Man, it's been years."

Wes had no memory of Jay Meacham. He had very few memories of anything that happened to him before Deacon got custody of him when he was eight, but he doubted *Jay* knew him from that long ago. Deacon wouldn't have forgotten to tell him that the mayor of Kirkland was actually their long-lost cousin.

Jay must have noticed his confusion. "I met you after the last game your first season at Western U. I'm an alum, too. Big supporter of the basketball team."

Wes still didn't remember meeting the mayor, but he remembered that game, in particular one of the sweetest three-pointers he'd shot in his life. He wasn't much of a jumper, but he'd had springs in his legs that night and he'd scored right over the head of the defender from the Cardinals team.

"Nice to see you again," Wes said.

The tall woman he'd seen before passed the open door again and then paused. She stood behind the mayor, but since she was about six inches taller than him, she had a perfect view into the room.

"That was some game," Jay said, oblivious to the woman. "You had twenty-eight points." He'd been holding a baseball cap by his side, and now he put it on. "You signed my T-shirt that night. Mind signing my hat now?"

He bent his head as he handed Wes a Sharpie. "I'll have a whole Wes Fallon outfit."

Wes took the Sharpie and stared down at the guy. His neck was bent and Wes noticed that the skin there was sunburned. In college he'd gotten a huge kick out of signing stuff for people. In Madrid, it was part of his job. He was retired now. *And this?* This was just awkward.

Ryan turned slightly to the side, straightening one of the perfectly aligned stacks of paper on his desk, and Wes was grateful to him. The woman watched intently. He wondered for a second if she was Trish Jones, but she was much too young.

The mayor was still waiting.

The woman crossed her arms.

"You want to take the hat off?" he tried.

"I don't want to put you to any trouble. Just go ahead and sign it on the brim."

Because signing a hat while it's on another man's head isn't awkward and uncomfortable at all.

He made the mistake of looking at the woman again. She stared right back, waiting to see what he would do. She knew how idiotic this was.

It was a stroke of freaking amazing luck that Jay had followed Wes's college career and what he needed to do was to capitalize on that connection regardless of how it made him feel. For Deacon.

Wes uncapped the Sharpie and pinched the brim of the hat between his fingers to hold it steady. He felt Jay's breath on his hand as he rushed an illegible scrawl across the brim. When he was finished, he tapped Jay on the head with the pen. And if he wasn't so careful about tapping lightly, well, maybe the mayor would re-

member to take his hat off the next time he asked someone for an autograph. "Done."

"I have to say, I'm thrilled you're here!" Jay clapped
his hands. "Your brother must be pleased you're available."

When he realized what he'd said, Jay flushed right
to his hairline, the color on his face matching his bright
red neck. "Not that anyone would be pleased about your
injury or your—"

"It's okay, Jay. I'm happy to be in Kirkland. Deacon and I are both looking forward to the possibilities."

The woman stepped into the office. Her legs were a
mile long in tight blue jeans and Wes was distracted by
an entirely different set of possibilities.

Ryan noticed her and waved her forward. "Mayor
Meacham, we have another visitor."

The mayor didn't seem to hear him. "Did Ryan tell
you about our lunchtime basketball league on Wednes-
days? I told him to tell you." Jay punched him lightly
on the biceps. "We'll help you keep in shape now that
you're a civilian."

Based on how tight the muscle in his jaw looked,
Wes was pretty sure Ryan was suppressing the urge to
punch the mayor.

"I'd love to join," he said. "Send me the details."

Wes Fallon, small-town rec-league guy. Fabi would
have a field day if she knew.

Ryan stepped around the mayor and said to the
woman, "Can I help you?"

"I'm Posy Jones. I have an appointment with Mr. Fallon."

Posy Jones. Her voice was rich and throaty in a way that made Wes think of late nights in dark bars. He tried not to notice how long her dark eyelashes were or the way her eyes seemed lit with humor.

"Posy," Jay said. "I haven't seen you in a while. Did you come with your mother?"

"My mother isn't available today." But she didn't offer any additional details.

Not available? Where exactly was Trish Jones and the Fallon Foundation's sixty-eight thousand dollars?

An awkward silence fell over the room. Everyone seemed to be waiting for someone else to ask that exact question.

A weak person would have leaped to fill the silence, but Posy kept her mouth shut and her expression blank. As if she'd just informed them that the special of the day was apple pie but she really didn't care one way or the other if they ordered it.

If something was up with the money, he would find out, but he didn't want the mayor, or worse yet, his eager and überprofessional assistant to hear.

His brother had built the next phase of plans for his Fallon Foundation Centers around the Hand-to-Hand programs. Nothing mattered more to him than this venture. If there was something fishy with Trish's unofficial fundraiser, it had the potential to ruin the goodwill of the town of Kirkland.

He owed Deacon a debt he could never repay, but he

would keep trying. Whatever was going on with Posy Jones, her mom and this fundraiser, he'd put it straight.

POSY WAS AT an enormous disadvantage and she knew it even before she walked into that office and got her first glimpse of Wes Fallon in the flesh. As it were.

Seeing the mayor suck up to Wes made her sweat. There'd be no hometown advantage here for her mother.

Her only option was to bluff…hard…until her mom came back with the cash.

She knew Jay Meacham mostly by reputation, but she had met him a few times at downtown business-booster events she'd attended with her mom. He wasn't exactly a thought leader, but he got the job done and kept people happy. In a town like Kirkland where the citizens were involved and motivated, the mayor needed to be better at making friends than he was at making policy.

It had been bad enough that Chloe Chastain would be thrilled to expose Trish as a swindler. On top of that, her mom had stolen from a charity that actually seemed to do good work. Watching Wes sign a hat for the mayor brought it home that he and his brother were both minor celebrities. Her mom didn't stand a chance if she got caught.

"I think Posy and I should head to my office," Wes said. "Nice to meet you, guys. See you on the courts."

He seemed to remember the T-shirt in his hand. "I brought you a shirt, Jay. Almost forgot to give it to you."

Jay thanked him much more sincerely than was necessary for a white T-shirt that wasn't even autographed.

Then Wes was right up close to her and she registered just how tall he was. At least six-six. She'd known the number, feet and inches, from her internet...research... but pictures and a few statistics had done a terrible job of preparing her for Wes in real life. His shoulders alone, broad and straight, deserved their own section in Google. She was used to looking down at people or looking even tall men in the eye, but Wes was a good six inches taller than her and built on a large scale. The dark stubble on his jaw and a military-style buzz cut made him look older and more commanding than the long, thick dark hair he'd had in his photos.

She swallowed.

Puppy Pete would have dropped to his belly if Wes loomed over him like this, but Posy straightened her shoulders, happy for once that they made her look even bigger.

Bluff. Hard. Game time.

"I don't mean to interrupt. If you and the mayor want to talk about basketball, I can wait in your office." She smiled her professional helpless-lady smile, all teeth and bright eyes with a deferential tilt to her head. When she went incognito on quality control visits for her job, that smile came in handy for assessing concierge service. Some men fell right into that particular smile and never noticed that she was grading them on everything from their attitude to their knowledge of the local hot spots.

"I think we're about finished," Wes said easily. "But thanks."

He had not fallen for the clueless smile.

He motioned for her to go first and then followed her out and down the hall.

"I'm sorry I didn't bring a hat," she said, switching tactics on the chance his ego was big enough to let her distract him. "I didn't realize you'd be signing merchandise."

He glanced down at her. "It's probably better you didn't have one."

"Really?"

He stopped in front of a door and opened it. "Yup. I charge five bucks for an autograph. I only did the mayor's for free because he's an old friend."

Her eyes widened. His ego was that big he charged for his autograph?

"Somebody has to keep me in solid-gold sneakers."

When she'd seen him sign the hat, she'd actually hoped he might be a dumb jock. It would have made her job so much easier. But, true to form, she could not catch a break. Wes was sharp. And funny. And capable of laughing at himself.

"Good to know. I'll bring a five when I bring my hat."

"Until then, maybe you'd like a shirt or a sticker." He bent toward a box near his desk, and shallow, objectifying creature that she was, she admired the view. Wes knew how to wear a pair of jeans.

He handed her the promo items and she thanked him.

There was only one chair in the room and it was behind the desk. She didn't know quite what to do so she stood near the window, pretending to look at the park while she gathered her thoughts.

Wes leaned on the desk at the front of the office, his long legs stretched in front of him and arms crossed on his chest. "My brother and I wanted to thank your mom for her efforts on behalf of the Fallon Foundation." Apparently they were finished joking around. "The money she raised is going to make a difference to a lot of kids."

She felt as if she was being lectured, but she reminded herself that he didn't know anything. He might be suspicious—in fact, she was now fairly certain he was suspicious—but he didn't know anything. Posy forced herself not to look at him. She was an innocent woman, admiring the view of the parking lot.

"My mom is a very kind person. I'm sure she'll be thrilled to meet you. Unfortunately, she's been called out of town."

"So you brought the check?"

CHAPTER FOUR

SHE PULLED HERSELF together. He was good-looking, but she'd known that going in. If he was also sharp, that only meant she had to be even more on her game. What she cared about was keeping him distracted and semi-satisfied until her mom returned.

"She wants to give you the money in person. She's very eager to meet you and your brother."

"In person, huh?" He straightened his back. "My brother said your mom's been out of touch for a couple days. Is everything okay?"

"With my mother?" Posy pulled the strap of her bag tighter across her shoulder, praying her voice would hold steady. "She's fine."

"Oh, good to know. I thought she might be sick or having some other kind of trouble."

"No." She needed to give him the file she'd brought and get out of here. "She was called out of town unexpectedly to visit my aunt. She asked me to watch her store and dog-sit—and keep this appointment with you. She'll be back in a few days and she really wants to meet you both."

It was mostly the truth.

Her cell was in her bag. If only it would ring with

a call from her mom to tell her the wire was going through.

"I read your website last night," she blurted out. "I really admire the work you're doing. Kirkland is lucky you guys are coming here."

Wes raised his eyebrows and smiled, and she was surprised to find herself smiling back at him. She'd never actually experienced an infectious smile before.

"The foundation is all my brother. This is my first day on the job and all I've done so far is sign a hat."

She was definitely going to have to watch out for this guy. Good-looking, charming and sure to file a police report if he found out what her mom had been up to with her checkbook in the back room of Wonders.

Time for phase two of her bluff.

She'd considered trying to skate along for the next few days without giving him any information, but then she'd decided a better plan would be to give him too much of the wrong sort. If she had any luck, he would be so overwhelmed by the thorough records her mom had kept that he wouldn't care that she was a few days late with the check.

"My mom did make you a list of donors and all the amounts. Everything is categorized and you can see where and how they donated." She handed Wes a one-inch binder stacked with printed pages. "She asked me to deliver this."

"Thanks." He opened the binder and flipped the pages, then glanced behind him at the one chair. "I'm not set up for meetings yet." He ducked behind his desk and grabbed a basketball out of the bag on the floor. "There are tables outside near the court. How would you feel about moving this conversation outside?"

She would feel a heck of a lot better if they ended the conversation, instead.

"I'm not sure what we'd have to meet about, Wes."

"We're meeting about the foundation." He tapped the binder. "All the money these people donated. I thought I'd get to thank your mom, but since she's not here, looks like you're on the hook."

Wes dribbled the ball once, the long muscles in his arms flexing as he caught the ball again with unconscious skill. The smack of the ball on the tile floor echoed in the empty office. "You ready?"

She closed her mouth. *Bluff. Hard.* She had a job to do here and it had nothing to do with Wes's many physical charms.

CHAPTER FIVE

"PEOPLE ARE AMAZING," Wes said. "Look how many are for less than twenty bucks." They'd spread Posy's binder out on a picnic table under a tree that was covered in pink blossoms. The petals kept drifting down onto the paper. He brushed his hand across the page, knocking another blossom to the ground.

"It's been a remarkable experience for my mom." Her voice had lost the no-nonsense tone. There was something going on with Posy, he thought.

She'd had one foot out the door since they stepped into his office, but Wes wasn't about to let her off that easy. For one thing, he didn't think she was telling him everything she knew. Posy was all business when they were going over the details, but he'd seen a quick flash or two of uncertainty, mostly when he'd said anything touching on the subject of her mom.

She closed the binder and slid it across the table closer to him.

"What about the other blogger?" he asked, refusing to take her big hint that their meeting was over. "Chloe, right?"

"Chloe Chastain."

"She and your mom are an unbeatable team. Do you know her?"

"We grew up together."

"So Kirkland is the ultimate hometown—everybody helps everybody else."

"I left a long time ago," Posy said. "But don't believe everything you hear."

He'd assumed she lived in town. Why was she here, otherwise? "You don't live in Kirkland?"

"Rochester. I'm a quality control inspector for the Hotel Marie chain."

"Quality control? Now I'm imaging you checking in with a fake name and making all kinds of crazy requests to see if the staff is up to snuff."

"We call them personas, not 'fake names.' And my requests are always reasonable."

"Extra towels, not chocolate fountains?"

Had Wes ever ordered a chocolate fountain? Maybe with one of those beautiful women she'd seen in the pictures last night. She stared at a pink petal on the table next to her pinky.

"Look, Wes," Posy said as she stood, "I'm staying at my mom's house so I can watch her dog. I'm in charge of her store, and I really should at least check my work email while I'm here. You've got all the data and as soon as my mom gets back, she's dropping off a check. That's about all I can tell you."

She was brushing him off. Definitely something strange going on. Wes went into foster care when he was two and came out when he was eight. In those six years, he'd been bounced from five separate placements. He didn't remember the details about many of them, but he'd learned to tell when someone was lying to him.

"I'm just going to say this and you can say what you know and we can move on, okay?"

She flinched. Not much, but he saw it.

"The situation seems off to me. Not just to me, frankly. Chloe Chastain had some questions for my brother. Your mom is sitting on a lot of money she raised in our name," he said. "Our reputation is on the line and we're still negotiating here in Kirkland."

"I'm not surprised you have questions, but my mom will deliver your money. I promise."

She didn't flinch that time. She met his eyes, and he couldn't make himself call her a liar. He didn't want her to be a liar.

"Well, I'm looking forward to meeting her," he said. "My brother put his heart and soul into the Fallon Foundation, and this new project in Kirkland means everything to him. Neither of us could believe that your mom, a stranger, would go out of her way to do this kind of fundraising. He's floored and so am I. People like her don't get enough credit."

POSY DIDN'T WANT HIM to say nice things about her mom. She didn't want him to say nice things about anything. She wanted to not like him and for him to work for some horrible corporation. Not a foundation that did good for the community. She didn't want to respect him, because she had to keep lying to him.

She hated lying and the longer she talked to Wes, the more she hated herself. She shouldn't have let herself get dragged into her mother's mess. She knew better. This was the last time. It had to be.

"You play basketball?" he asked.

She waited for the obligatory comment about her height, but it didn't come. He just waited for her to answer.

"I did."

"High school? College?"

"Both."

"I did, too," he offered as he leaned down and grabbed the ball from the ground. "High school, college, then in Europe. But I got hit by a truck so I'm retired now."

When he mentioned his accident, he touched a spot on his head behind his right ear. She noticed the scar there, a thin line of red flesh visible through the dark stubble.

"I read about the accident." He looked up. "Google. I was trying to get ready for our meeting. I'm sorry."

"A dog ran into the road," he said.

"The articles didn't mention that."

He lifted one shoulder. "It was a little dog."

Wes was getting more dangerous by the second. Pete hadn't understood humor.

"So this job with the foundation, where does it take you after Kirkland?"

"It's only a temporary gig. My brother asked me for help and I was at loose ends. It worked out." He touched his scar.

Funny that they'd both been thrown into this through an obligation to family.

"Want to shoot around?" he asked.

She stared up at him. He was serious. "Play basketball with you?"

"I just moved to town," he said. "I don't know any of the other boys yet."

He dribbled the ball deliberately while giving her that slow, sweet smile. He knew what he was doing with that smile.

Which irritated her. She was supposed to get in and get out. She'd had to buy a three-hole punch just to make that binder full of papers. She wasn't supposed to hang around and shoot baskets with him.

"I was in Mayor Meacham's office when you signed up for his lunchtime league."

"Well, he's not here right now." He caught the ball and without the rhythmic pounding, the playground was too quiet. He leaned toward her, tilting his head. "Besides, I want to play with you."

Oh. In that case.

"Come on, Posy. I'll go easy on you."

She'd been sitting at the picnic table, but now she stood. He was close enough for her to feel the height difference and to see the strength in his shoulders and arms. Wes might be named after a skinny *Star Trek* geek, but he was…well… There was a reason basketball players had as many groupies as rock stars. And her best fantasies had always been about guys who were built on a bigger scale, guys who were broad and tall and strong. Like Wes.

On the first day of school, her kindergarten teacher lined the class up by height to teach a lesson about big and small. Posy was the tallest kid in line. She towered over most of the girls and had a half inch or so even on the two boys in the class who were already six because they'd been held back. She'd been so proud to be the tallest kid, to have something no one else did that was hers all alone. That day on the playground at lunchtime, the girls were all pretending to be fairy princesses, but Chloe Chastain told her she couldn't be a fairy and made her be the giant instead. That was the first time she realized her height didn't make her special, it made her abnormal. She'd thrown herself into the game, though, and been such a successful giant that one of her classmates had to go to the nurse after she burst into tears and hyperventilated. Her mom had been so disappointed. She'd known she'd done something wrong but hadn't understood what.

Here on this playground with Wes, she didn't feel quite so out of step.

"Okay," she said, taking the ball from him. "I'll play you. But don't even think about going easy on me."

His smile widened, no longer the flirty weapon he used so well. She'd been with him for less than an hour and already she'd seen the serious businessman, the professional flirt, and now, a guy who looked as if he'd be an awful lot of fun at a water park.

He jogged to the foul line, clapped and held his hands out.

"I'm the new guy. I get first ball."

"I'm the lady. We'll shoot for it." She tossed it back to him and to prove she had manners said, "You can go first. Since you're the new guy."

While he set up for his shot, she took a long look at his…form. She had no chance in this contest. He went up for the shot and she bent to pull the laces on her sneakers tighter. The ball clanged off the metal rim of the hoop and she looked up, confused. How the hell had he missed that shot? He was staring at her. When her eyes met his, he shook himself and went to get the ball. *Ah.*

His miss gave her confidence, so she squared up to the basket and shot. Her ball sank so sweetly the net barely fluttered.

It might be the last shot she made, but it felt good.

HE COULDN'T BELIEVE he'd missed his shot.

He'd had it completely under control and then Posy leaned over to tie her shoe. A perfect view down the front of her shirt. She was wearing a lacy, hot-pink bra. *Pink.*

He was still getting a handle on Posy, but he hadn't figured her for a pink kind of person. Since it practically smoldered against her dark skin, he figured hot pink was a very, very good call.

When she sank her shot, she arched one black eyebrow at him and the corners of her mouth went up in a smile that she tried to hide. He knew the feeling—no matter how trapped he'd felt by his life while he was a pro, he'd never stopped loving the game. When things went right on the court, the power felt amazing.

She took the ball out at half court and waited for him to get set. Then she checked it to him and he passed it back. Her pass had been quick and accurate. He wasn't going to play her hard, but he was glad she'd been telling the truth about knowing how to play.

While he was thinking about how to keep the game close without letting her catch on that he wasn't going more than half speed, she darted past him, hell-bent for the hoop.

She was a lot faster than he expected and she'd caught him entirely flat-footed. He took off after her. He could make excuses all day but it wouldn't change the fact that she put an easy layup in while he was half a step behind her.

Another quick smile flashed across her face and the ball felt uncomfortable in his hands as he realized she was pretty. Not gorgeous like Fabi, but fresh. Like someone you'd see in a Coke commercial.

She checked the ball to him and settled in to play defense and the smile was gone as quickly as it had come. She didn't mean to lose without a fight. Okay, maybe not a Coke commercial for Posy, Nike was more her speed. He glanced at her again and her dark eyes tracked him.

Maybe instead of commercials, she could host one of those shows where people stalked wild animals.

He didn't have a chance to consider any more about

her best match for product representation because he needed his attention on the game.

She wasn't as good as him, obviously. He had her by more than six inches and at least fifty pounds, for starters. He'd also been playing and practicing with a professional team right up until a month ago, so he was in near-peak shape. But she had no give. Wouldn't admit that she couldn't muscle through him.

With the aggression she was throwing his way, he sensed Posy was taking this game to his body because she was carrying that load of anger he'd seen earlier. This was a place she could let it out.

Sure, he could have backed off, but the first time she put her hand on his back and tried to shove him off his dribble, the impression of her fingers felt good. He was aware of the scent of her hair and after a few minutes, of her sweat. When she took the ball out for the third time, he saw a bead of moisture at the base of her throat, right where the tendons in her neck came together in a vulnerable V. The sweat slid down her neck, headed for that lacy bra and he missed her head fake. She scored again.

It hadn't been that long since he'd been with Fabi.

He was attracted to a woman who was playing him harder than he'd ever been played outside a professional game. And she didn't seem overly concerned if she hurt him during the process. Of all the screwed-up things he'd been turned on by, he was turned on by playing basketball with Posy.

He shook his head when she blew past him again

and then he settled down to play. Attraction or not, he wasn't going to let her beat him that easily.

THE FIRST TIME she bumped him, it was an accident. He was guarding her tight and she wanted to move him off the ball, but her elbow connected with his stomach more sharply than she intended. Ashamed that she'd let her frustration toward her mom bleed over onto her game, she immediately paused to apologize.

He stole the ball from her and put it in, obliterating the small lead she'd snagged with her first shot. He hadn't even *noticed* that she'd hit him despite the fact that her elbow stung from the contact.

Posy almost called time-out. She'd been apologizing for being too big, too rough, too *much* her whole life. Over and over she'd gotten the message that she wasn't just physically too big, she was too competitive and wanted too much. People got angry when she didn't keep herself in check.

Wes pumped his fist and pointed at her, glee, not anger, on his face. "You done?"

She shook her head, energy humming through her. *No.* No, she was most definitely not done. She was just getting started.

She took the ball and when he moved in to guard her, she bumped him again, not that much harder, but deliberately this time. She leaned into his chest with her shoulder and pushed off, registering his solid strength. Again, he didn't seem to notice. He didn't lose a step.

Her focus slipped and she double-dribbled. He could have called her on it, but he didn't.

He was *patronizing* her.

It reminded her that she was mad. He was going to win, but he was not going to hand her a freebie. When she shot, she bounced the ball off the backboard, missing on purpose and letting him get the rebound. Two could play the deliberate screwup game.

He was taking his time, dribbling with his back to her while she sweated to keep up with him. He could have skirted her and they both knew it. He was messing around, keeping things nice, the way her mom did. She wanted him to notice how hard she was working. She wanted him to get serious and *compete*.

This time she gave him a real shove, her hand low on his back. His skin was hot through the thin fabric of his shirt and she pushed harder than she should have, relishing the power in her body against his. Her fingers slid dangerously low over the waistband of his shorts.

He noticed that one, even though he didn't stumble. *Damn.* He put the ball through his legs and spun to face her. He kept up his dribble as he studied her, the same sharp intelligence in his eyes she'd noticed before when he was grilling her about her mom. It was the moment when she should have backed off. She didn't need him to think about her or her mom. She needed to be background, less than background, while she got her mother out of this mess. He spun again, putting his back to her, and then he backed up and looked at her over his shoulder as he slowed his dribble. Was he daring her to do it again?

Posy moved closer, drawn in against her will by his taunt. He picked up speed, but she stayed with him. She put one hand on his left shoulder and used the other to grab a handful of shirt near his hip. With a powerful twist, he pulled away and then dribbled past her, but not before she registered his biceps and the muscles in his waist flexing against her fingers.

He scored.

She didn't care. The focus of the game had changed. All she wanted was another opportunity to touch him. Playing this game with Wes, she wasn't an overgrown, overaggressive freak of nature. He was bigger and stronger and he could take everything she had to give. He didn't just take it, he asked for it. He wanted it. Wanted it all.

SHE WAS PLAYING DIRTY. Every time she connected with him, an elbow to the side, her foot on the instep of his shoe, her hand on his hip, he felt another jolt of adrenaline.

His skin was alive with electricity, anticipating her touch, and then jumping when it came. He was so turned on, it was hard to concentrate on the game, but when his focus slipped, she took advantage.

She kept upping the ante, hitting harder, holding more blatantly, almost as if she was daring him to stop her. But he didn't want to stop her.

He wasn't sure exactly what was going on, but he

knew he wasn't dominating her. It was as if he was absorbing her strength.

She was losing and he thought about pulling back and letting her win, but she didn't want a pass. His brother used to do that to him when he was little. He wouldn't insult Posy that way. He took a shot, jumping up and over her, but he missed, and not on purpose. He knocked down the rebound, but couldn't control it, and the ball careened away. She touched it, but missed and then dived as it headed out of bounds. She batted at the ball, driving it over her shoulder and directly into his nose. The ball bounced off his face and off the court, landing near her bag under the picnic table.

"Holy—" He clapped his hand over his face as blood dripped onto the toe of his shoe. "Out on me," he muttered. "I fully intend to finish kicking your butt as soon as I can staunch the bleeding."

He sat on the asphalt and pulled the neck of his shirt up to press against his nose. Sweat trickled down his back and dried on his legs, the chill reminding him that it was still early spring. Good. He needed to cool down.

She was quiet and he didn't know what to expect when he finally looked up. The Posy from the meeting—contained, cool and businesslike? Or the bold, antagonistic…sizzling woman he'd just been sweating with on the court.

He thought the blood might have stopped, so he risked tilting his head up. She had one hand over her mouth and he could swear he saw tears in her eyes.

Damn it. *His* face was hurt. Posy wasn't allowed to cry. Absolutely not.

"You arrange this kind of orientation for all the new Kirklanders?" he asked.

She didn't respond. She was so still, but tense and poised away as if she was about to bolt.

He patted the ground next to him. "Sit. It's making my neck hurt to look up at you." Deacon would kill him if he reactivated the concussion from the accident.

She sank onto the macadam near him, but not close. She bent her knees with her elbows propped across them. "I'm sorry," she said simply.

He touched his nose to confirm that the blood had stopped. It hadn't been much of a nosebleed in the end. A few spatters on the neck of his shirt. He lifted the hem and wiped it across his hand to get the blood off his fingers.

"Sorry," he repeated. He hoped she wasn't one of those people who got sick at the sight of blood.

"You're ruining your shirt."

"If I were an old guy, I'd have a handkerchief." He shrugged. "Guys my age have to use what we can find."

"But—"

"Damage is done." He dragged his shirt off over his head and wadded it up behind him. "Let's talk about what just happened."

She jerked backward. "I said I was sorry."

"No, I meant what happened between us."

She was on her feet almost before he finished speaking.

"I got caught up in the game," she said. Her eyes were fixed on a point just over his head.

"I got caught up, too," he said. But it hadn't been in the game.

"Listen, I have to go. My mom will be in touch as soon as she gets back. A few days at the most. You have my cell, but texting's better. Or email. Email is fine."

He pushed himself up.

"We don't have to talk about what it was. But I had a good time." He wanted to be sure she heard him. "Thanks."

She shrugged, picked up her bag and gave him a quick wave over her shoulder.

"Hey, Posy," he called. She stopped. "We're doing an Equipment Day on Sunday. It's this thing the Fallon centers do where they give sports gear away to kids. My brother and his wife will be here and we'd really like to thank the folks who ran the fundraiser. You think your mom will be back by then?"

"I'll find out," she said before walking away.

Well, he thought, *that was instructive.* Posy Jones was an enigma. A tall, aggressive, fierce enigma.

With really sexy taste in bras.

CHAPTER SIX

POSY LEFT THE PLAYGROUND with as much dignity as she could manage. Luckily, her role in quality assurance required her to occasionally act a part. She didn't look back at Wes as she walked to her Jeep. As soon as she was around the side of the building out of his sight, she picked up speed until she was jogging when she reached her parking spot.

She pulled out, allowing herself one glance toward the court where she saw Wes, stretched out full-length on the foul line. She shivered because, God help her, she wanted very badly to be stretched out under him.

Her cell phone rang and she grabbed it, hoping it would be her mom telling her everything was settled.

It was Maddy.

"I'm so glad you called. I just made a huge mistake."

"Did someone find out about the money?"

"No." Posy banged her fist on the steering wheel. "Not yet."

Maddy didn't answer right away. "Can you come out here to the Knoll?"

"I'd love to see you. What's up?"

"I'll tell you when you get here."

The Knoll was about ten minutes outside Kirkland.

It was a pretty drive, but Posy spent the whole time re-living the debacle of her game with Wes.

She asked at the desk and was told she could find her cousin in the grotto carved into the hillside under the main chapel. She took the outside route, walking down the shallow stone stairs while watching a pair of sisters pushing hand mowers across the lawn in front of the visitor center.

The air inside the grotto was cool and infused with the scent of the thousands of candles that had been burned there over years of services. Posy inhaled deeply. Ever since she'd been a little girl following the responses in the missal, the familiar traditions of spiritual ritual had calmed her.

"Posy," Maddy called softly. "I'm up here."

Her cousin, dressed in the loose woven pants and smock the sisters wore for work, was kneeling in front of the small altar at the left side of the grotto. Visitors lit candles there for special intentions and several were flickering in the dim light. Maddy had a case of candles open on the floor next to her and she was gently pry-ing spent stubs off the stone and replacing them with fresh ones. She and Maddy were the same age and had always been as close as sisters.

Maddy handed her a thin, metal paint scraper. "You want to help me work on these?"

Posy grabbed the tool and set to work on a candle stub in front of her. It wasn't as hard to remove as she'd expected and it flipped in the air when she shoved the scraper under it.

"Sorry," she said as she gathered the fallen candle and put it into the discard bucket.

Maddy slid her own scraper under a candle and lifted it out. "The reason I called—"

"Wait, can I tell you what happened with Wes first? If I don't spit it out now I won't be able to think."

Posy remembered the charge she'd gotten when she pushed her hand against Wes's back and he didn't move. Her hand slipped and she knocked a fresh candle flying. She managed to catch it before it hit the ground.

"Something happened with Wes?" Maddy asked. "Absolutely tell me that story."

"What? Why are you saying it like that?"

"Just… There's been a dry spell since Pete."

"It was recovery time. Pete was—"

"A nice guy, but not right for you."

"I was going to say a wimp and a subpar lover, but we can go with your phrasing if it fits in better with your duties as a professional nice person."

"I was nice long before I took my vows," Maddy said. "But we're talking about Wes."

She bent to get a new candle and Posy took the opportunity to rush out the story while her cousin wasn't looking at her.

"I went to see him. I was going to bluff him. Get in and get out."

"Get to the mistake, Posy. I'm dying."

"I think I came on to him…?"

Maddy raised her eyebrows and looked impressed. Posy stared at the lit candle in front of her, remembering how Wes's dark blue eyes mocked at her as he wiped the blood off his face with the hem of his T-shirt. Then she remembered the casual, but incredibly sexy way he took off his shirt and continued to sit there with every single muscle and contour of his body in view while they *chatted*.

"You…came on to him?"

"Can you talk about this stuff at work?" Posy asked, suddenly aware that they were in the grotto where the very air felt like church. "They don't monitor your conversations, do they?"

"The sisters are aware that people have sexual feelings, Posy. The vow is celibacy, not prudery. Tell me what happened."

"I was angry and feeling trapped by all this stuff with my mom, and Wes. He's, oh, man, you know the guy he is. He's handsome and successful, he just retired from playing professional basketball, and he knows how to use that smile. Five bucks says he was prom king in high school, the fraternity social chair and the guy every one of his girlfriends' moms was hoping they'd end up with. He's never struggled for anything in his life. Never not been loved. He's that guy. And you know that guy is never worth a second look."

"And yet, you came on to him."

"I know," Posy practically wailed. "He said we should shoot around so we did. He's tall, Maddy, and strong. I kept trying to push him around. And then I realized I didn't care so much about pushing him around. I mean, I wanted to push him around but it was because I wanted to touch him."

"Wow."

"Right."

She might be confessing to Maddy right now, and might be full of shame that she'd lost control, but later tonight, alone in her room, she'd be remembering exactly how he'd felt under her hands.

"So did he...respond? Reciprocate?" Maddy gave a short laugh. "Did you have to lock the gym doors?"

"We were outside.... I hit him in the face with the ball." Posy shuddered. She could hear the smack all over again. "It didn't break his nose. But there was blood."

Maddy dropped the candle she was holding and wrinkled her nose. "A bloody nose? In the middle of your big seduction? Oh, Posy."

Which got on his T-shirt. Which he'd taken off.

"Hard to keep up a seduction once there's blood," her cousin added.

"It wasn't even a seduction, though," Posy said. "I wasn't seducing him, it was—wild."

Posy wished she could roll the tape back and get a redo on the whole day. "I should have brought him a cupcake from the Lemon Drop or potpourri from Wonders."

"That's what I'm curious about," Maddy said. "You're good at covering up the parts of yourself that make you uncomfortable, but this guy brought it out." She put her hands on her knees and leaned forward. "Was he interested?"

Posy couldn't meet her cousin's eyes. She didn't want Maddy to know how badly she'd wanted Wes to be interested.

"That's beside the point," Posy said. "My mother stole from him."

"Can I meet Wes?"

"Why?"

"So I can have my evil way with him." Maddy rolled her eyes. "Because I want to meet the guy who let loose your wild side."

"I'm not going to repeat that performance."

"But I love your wild side."

Posy sighed.

Maddy put her scraper down and pulled a folded piece of paper out of her back pocket. "I'm glad you went first because I liked that story and there's a chance you're going to stop talking to me right now."

Posy waited.

"Your mom checked in this morning for a silent retreat. She gave me a note for you."

Maddy held the note out and Posy took it. It was the same thick paper with the Christmas border and Wonders logo she'd used for the first note. Was it only a few hours ago that Posy read that one and counted down the days until she'd be out of this trouble?

Dear Posy,
I'm sorry I lied to you. Aunt Denise wasn't able to
lend me the money, but I couldn't face telling you

that. I am going to continue my retreat until the
police come for me, unless you have a better idea.
Your loving mother,
Holly
P.S. Give Angel a kiss for me.

"Holly?"

"We allow our silent retreat guests to choose a name that's symbolic of their journey."

"What is she thinking? She's waiting for the police to get here? Does she know what happens after the police get to you? Can you imagine my mom in jail? No," Posy said. "I have to fix this."

Maddy took the note from her and read it through. "You don't *have* to fix it."

"I should let my mom go to jail?"

"Your life isn't your own as long as you're being pulled back into hers every few months." Maddy put her scraper down and set another candle into a spot on the rocky shelf in front of her. Then she faced Posy. "I think you're afraid of yourself. You've spent your whole life trying to be smaller and less competitive and more like the daughter Trish thought she wanted. Someone who fit in and didn't make waves and kept everything nice. But something about this guy stirred up the real Posy. You have a chance to get to know a guy who might be really good for you. Tell him the truth and let your mom work this out herself. Don't let her stand in your way."

Posy's palms felt hot and beads of sweat appeared on her forehead.

"If he wasn't scared by you, maybe it's time for you to figure out why you are."

"Maybe he's a kinky weirdo who likes the taste of his own blood."

"Maybe," Maddy said. "Or maybe he wasn't scared because he's a guy who likes a woman who knows what she wants and isn't afraid to fight for it. Your mom is hiding out here, Posy, hoping everything will work out somehow. Are you hiding, too?"

"It's not that easy, Maddy."

"I was there right with you when we were kids and you were always on the outside. I know how hard Trish made it for you because she doesn't understand you. But you're twenty-eight. You need someone to stand up to you—someone strong enough to stand with you." Maddy touched her shoulder. "Maybe Wes isn't that guy. But you deserve to find out."

"I can't let my mom go to jail," Posy said. "I'm going to help her one more time and then that's it. I'm going to get a loan to cover this and pay myself back when I sell the house."

"You're sure?"

"I don't know what else to do."

Maddy hugged her. "I have a little money. A bit more than three thousand dollars. Let me lend it to you."

Posy hated taking her cousin's money, but she was in no shape to turn down a loan.

"Thank you. I'll pay you back as soon as I can. Where is my mom? I need to talk to her."

"She's requested no visitors and no calls. I can't let

you in." Her cousin's mouth twisted and she sighed. "It's my job to help her set boundaries around her retreat."

Which Trish would know. She was using Maddy as a shield. "She knows I won't get you in trouble. Can you deliver a note?"

Maddy took a pen out of her back pocket. Posy flipped the note from her mom over and wrote:

> *Dear Mom,*
> *I will pay the Fallons their money. Don't tell anyone what you did. I suppose that won't be difficult while you're on your SILENT RETREAT. I would appreciate it if you could wrap your retreat up quickly so you can come home and help me deal with your house and Wonders.*
>   *If you don't, I'm selling everything.*
> *Love,*
> *Posy*

WHEN POSY DROVE BACK to her mom's house, she kept the radio off. She wasn't really crying, but for some reason, tears kept leaking down her cheeks. Every time one escaped, she rubbed it away with the heel of her hand, rubbing hard. She didn't want this. Didn't want any of it. Her mom's mess was enough, but now she'd met a guy she really liked who was making her look deeper at herself—and her mother—than she was prepared to look.

She opened the front door and waited for Angel to rush her. When the dog didn't appear, Posy wondered if she was lying in ambush somewhere, ready to leap out from under a chair to attack her ankles or steal something else from her bag. But the dog still didn't appear when she poured kibble into her bowl in the kitchen. She kicked the bowl a few times to make the food rattle, but no Angel.

"I don't like your poodle games, Angel!" she called. There was no answer from the silent house. No skittering of tiny toenails on the floor of the hall.

She walked through the house and finally, in the laundry room, found a window where the screen had been pushed out from the inside. She pulled the curtain to the side.

She was shocked to see Angel staring back at her from under a fern near the grill on the edge of the patio. She went back to the kitchen and opened the door to call Angel. The dog came out from under the plants, her head cocked to one side. Angel's mixed heritage was most evident in her mismatched ears, one of which flopped neatly and obediently forward. The other ear stuck straight out to the side, the long fringes of fur flying from the edges giving it the appearance of a medieval battle flag.

That one wild ear swiveled and Angel took a step toward Posy. She had a piece of shiny red fabric clutched in her teeth.

"What in the name of heaven is that?"

Posy stepped out onto the porch.

The dog dropped the fabric, barked once and took off running through the Nickersons' yard next door—her white fur glowing in the late-evening setting sun.

Posy found a twig on the porch and used it to lift the fabric. It was a bra. Victoria's Secret red satin with a clothespin still hanging from one strap.

For half a second she considered trying to find the bra's owner, but couldn't face the thought. She slid it off the stick into the garbage can at the corner of the house.

Her mom was in hiding. The dog was stealing lingerie. Posy was left holding down the ranch house.

Perfect.

EARLY THE NEXT MORNING, she sat at the counter in the kitchen and went over her own finances. She was a diligent saver, but unfortunately she'd just pumped almost all her money into a down payment on a condo in Rochester. The rest of her money was tied to her 401(k) account, which meant a penalty if she robbed it to pay the Fallons back. She did have a twenty-thousand-dollar line of credit that she'd opened because she wanted to upgrade the kitchen in her new place. She could use that, plus a few thousand she had in her emergency savings and the three from Maddy.

She called a dealer and set up an appointment for later that afternoon to get an estimate on the collections at her mom's house. If he liked what he saw and he gave her any kind of decent offer, she'd ask for a check right there. At this point, she didn't care about getting good value for any of her mom's stuff. She just wanted to sell it, pay this money back and move forward.

As soon as her bank opened, she was on the phone with the mortgage department. Luckily, the loan officer who'd done her mortgage thought she would be able to qualify for an additional loan. Unfortunately, it would take more than a week for the paperwork to go through.

She was on her way to fixing things, but it wasn't going to be soon enough. The Fallons wanted to include the fundraiser acknowledgment in their event on Sunday. She wasn't going to be able to raise the whole amount in a day and a half.

She heard a soft thump from the laundry room and then she heard the tapping of Angel's toenails on the hardwood floor. The dog stopped in the doorway to the kitchen, a long, black snake clutched in her jaws.

Posy jumped on top of her chair and pointed at the dog and snake. "Get that thing out of here, right now. Out! Go!"

As usual, Angel did the exact opposite of her command, walking farther into the kitchen, dragging the snake, which she now realized was actually not a snake, but the tail of something whose body lay out of view behind the dog in the other room.

"That better not be a dead animal," Posy said. She sniffed the air. At least it wasn't a skunk.

Angel opened her mouth and let the tail drop on the floor before crossing the room to drink out of her water bowl. Posy climbed off her chair and approached the dead thing carefully, prepared to run if it should twitch or moan or in any way offer evidence that it wasn't actually dead. Within about three steps, though, she realized it wasn't the tail of a dead thing. It was a strap. The purse was what was out of view in the other room.

Posy spun around and spotted the dog curled in her bed near the sliding doors. Angel's white tail was tucked across her nose, but her shiny eyes were watching.

"You're a very bad dog," she muttered as she picked the purse up. "But your taste in handbags is exquisite." Angel had brought home a gorgeous Burberry satchel-style purse—easily a five-hundred-dollar-plus purchase.

Posy dug inside and pulled out a matching Burberry wallet and found a driver's license. *Chloe Chastain.*

A quick flash of white and Angel was standing next to the cupboard where Trish kept her dog snacks.

Was it possible she was going mental? The dog definitely didn't steal Chloe's purse on purpose because she knew Posy needed money. People didn't even carry money in their purses anymore, did they?

Chloe lived right across the street. Posy briefly wondered about that red bra but then shuddered. She had enough on her mind without adding Chloe's taste in underwear to the mix.

She glanced in the dollar-bill section of the wallet and saw a thick sheaf of twenties. A few hundred dollars, at least. Chloe must have been on her way to poker night. Or a ransom drop.

She snapped the wallet shut and dropped it into the bag.

Angel scratched at the cupboard door.

"You're selling yourself short, working for treats," she said. "Next time bring me her ATM code, and I'll take you out for a steak."

She got a biscuit and handed it to Angel, who took it gently from her hand and then zipped back to her bed.

Posy sat at the counter, looking from her financial notes, to the purse to the wallet. She had to figure out how to return Chloe's bag without seeing or being seen by the other woman.

CHAPTER SEVEN

"THAT'S A DAISY," Mrs. Meacham said. "Don't pull it."

Wes gave the green shoot a skeptical look. He was far from an expert gardener, but he did know what a daisy looked like. How did she know which of the green stems sticking up out of the ground was a weed and which was a daisy?

"I planted those daisies in 1973, a few days before my daughter was born," Mrs. Meacham explained. "I was nine months pregnant, kneeling in the dirt. It took me ten minutes just to get down there and another ten to get back up." She sniffed. "It's a daisy."

Mrs. Meacham knew what she was talking about, he figured, so he moved on and pulled up a clump of grass, carefully avoiding another green stem thing that looked like the one Mrs. M. just said was a daisy.

"Good job."

He avoided another daisy.

"Don't you have anything you need to do at your apartment?" she asked. "Seems like even if the place is furnished, you'd want to get settled."

"I'm settled," he said. "Everything looks great."

Before he got to town, Deacon had asked Jay Meacham if he knew any furnished places for rent. Jay had connected them with his mother and Wes moved into the apartment over her garage.

He liked Mrs. M. and he was happy she was letting him help her with her weeding. Not because he was planning to take up gardening anytime soon, but because he'd seen how much effort it meant for her to walk up and down the three steps leading to her back door. She'd never have been able to bend over to do this job.

Wes had never lived alone before. In college, he'd lived with his buddy, Oliver, and then after he graduated, he'd shared a place with a group of his teammates. He'd never felt permanent in Madrid. He hadn't expected to get cut necessarily, but he'd never committed to Europe by buying a place the way some of the other guys from the States did. He'd been happy enough to share an apartment with a couple guys and then spend his off-season with Deacon and Julia.

His brother and sister-in-law took in foster kids, mostly older teenagers who were pretty close to being independent, so the roster of people living with them was constantly changing anyway. They said they liked having him and had set aside a room that they kept empty for him. Well, mostly empty. Sometimes when a kid needed an emergency placement and the rest of the house was full, they used Wes's room, but he didn't mind sleeping on the couch. If he did get bothered, he could just go to a hotel. He never had gone to a hotel, though, because he actually liked being in the middle of Deacon and Julia's hectic family life.

Being alone was the thing he didn't really like.

He'd only been in Mrs. Meacham's apartment for two days and he'd already figured out that the time around dinner really dragged if you lived alone in a small town. At least, it did for him.

And apparently for Mrs. M., as well. Neither of them had made any kind of formal statement, but the past two nights, they'd spent an hour or so working on her yard. To be technically accurate, he worked on her yard and she bossed him around. But she was eighty-seven years old. No one could have expected her to push a wheel-barrow or shovel mulch, let alone crawl around pulling weeds out of the daisy bed, could they? She was the one who knew what needed doing and he was the one who didn't have arthritis, so their division of labor made sense.

"Do you know Posy Jones?" he asked.

He'd been thinking about Posy ever since she left the day before. He didn't know what he'd expected, but she'd been a surprise start to finish. Top to very sexy bottom.

"Trish Jones's daughter?" she asked.

He pulled another clump of grass and then scooped the pile he'd made into the mesh container she used to collect the waste. Later, he'd dump it in her compost pile. "That's her."

"I know her mother. Posy's the tall one, right?"

"Right." Tall and bossy. And a fan of hot-pink lacy bras.

"She moved away in high school sometime. Her parents were divorced and she went to live with her dad. I don't think Trish ever forgave either of them for that."

"Was she a bad mother?"

Mrs. M. sniffed. "Hard to say who's a bad mother. Bad for Posy, maybe. Her dad died three years ago, but she still comes to see her mom. Couldn't be all bad."

Wes knew firsthand that you couldn't tell from looking at someone what their childhood had been like. He didn't exactly go around telling people that the year he was born, his dad froze to death outside their trailer because he was too drunk to make it all the way to the door. He didn't mention the foster homes he'd been put into and he certainly didn't mention the ones he'd been kicked out of or the reasons why. When he talked about being a kid, he kept his stories strictly to the time after he turned eight when Deacon got drafted into the NBA and became his guardian. He had enough good stories from that part of his life—no need to get into the not-so-good ones from before.

"Her mom did a big fundraiser for the foundation," he said. "I met Posy yesterday."

"You liked her?"

Wes pulled another clump of weeds. "She seemed very competent."

The earphones for his iPod fell out of his pocket and he tried to hook them over his finger so he could slide them back in without getting dirt all over his clothes.

Mrs. M. reached and pulled the whole thing, headphones and iPod, out.

"My grandson has one of these. He thinks I should get one."

"Yeah? How old is your grandson?"

"Nine." She held it up. "Show me how to turn this on. Maybe he's right. I wouldn't have to get up and down all the time to change the channel if I could carry my music around with me."

"Um. Sure." He stood, brushing off the knees of his jeans and then wiping his hands across his seat. "Let me find a song you'll like."

"Something safe for the old lady, Wes?" She looked at him over the top of her red-frame glasses. Sometimes it was tough to tell if she was kidding. "That's censorship, son."

"But—"

She held out her hand. He helped her settle the earphones, his fingers brushing against the soft, wiry curls over her ears. He'd never touched an older woman's hair before and he was surprised by how thin it was. Everything about her was tiny—her little bird bones had concerned him earlier when he saw her coming down the back steps alone.

When the earphones were in, he pushed the play button and hoped none of the more explicit songs he used during warm-ups with his team came on. She smiled and nodded her head to the music. He craned his neck to see what was playing.

"My grandson likes Taylor Swift, too," she said, a little louder than normal.

"The girl I was dating bought that," he muttered. "It's on there because she used my account."

Mrs. M. kept nodding her head. "It's too bad they didn't think to include a delete button. People have to keep all this music they don't listen to." She winked at him. "How do you turn it up?"

He showed her how to work the controls and the volume and then went back to weeding. The yard wasn't that big. Mrs. Meacham's was an oddly shaped lot, so it had a large front yard, but back here was almost all taken up by a flagstone patio and the small garden. A chain-link fence bounded the garden on the four sides. The small gate was propped open by a stone statue of a dog.

"You want me to see if I can fix this gate?"

She didn't seem to hear him, so he repeated himself a little louder.

"You don't have to do things like that for me, Wes."

She took the earphones out and wrapped them around the iPod before she handed it back to him.

"Maybe it's not for you. Maybe I'm ashamed to live in a house with a shabby fence." He stood up. Mrs. M. really was a tiny little thing, although she swore she'd been taller in her heyday.

"The gate doesn't matter anymore. Molly is holding the gate open—she's past the time when I have to worry about her making an escape."

Wes looked at the stone dog more closely. It looked like a beagle and now he saw the inscription in the base: Molly. She'd died two years before.

"Molly was your dog?"

"The last in a long line."

"You're not getting another one?"

"No. I'm afraid I'm not up to the daily walks. I'd have to get some kind of horrible lapdog and the two of us would be old and fat together. That's not the kind of dog I like."

"I always wanted a dog," Wes said.

She didn't like to be coddled, but when she headed back on the short path to the house, he walked next to her. He took her right arm, folding it over his, and patted her hand. She wouldn't turn down his arm if it was gallantry, she'd told him last night.

He waited while she got in the back door of the house. She turned to him and said through the screen, "I don't mind if you want to have a dog out there in the apartment. As long as you clean up after it. I'd like to see a dog in the yard again. If you were serious."

He'd tried to save that dog in Madrid. Would he have brought it home if he'd caught it? He flinched as he remembered the impact of the truck.

He *had* always wanted a dog. There were a lot of things he'd wished for when he was a kid. He'd wanted to live with Deacon. That wish finally came true. He'd wanted to make Deacon proud. He'd done his best with basketball and he was working as hard as he could on the Hand-to-Hand project. He'd wished for the kind of suburban house he'd seen on TV with a basketball hoop in the driveway and a wreath on the front door that his wife changed for every season. He'd wished for someone who'd want to be his wife. Someone to have kids with.

He scooped up the container and dumped it in the compost pile. He ran a hand over the top of his head. The buzz continued to feel unfamiliar, continued to bring him back to those last days in Madrid and the accident.

When he was a kid, he'd had big dreams. Now he was an adult and he wasn't sure what he wanted.

He went up to his apartment. The place was so quiet, he'd started leaving the TV on for company. He turned on *SportsCenter* and then sat on the couch and opened his laptop. He pulled out the list of community groups they'd invited to the Equipment Day they were running on Sunday, and made sure he had a solid estimate of the number of kids each one was bringing. This was the first event the Hand-to-Hand program was holding in Kirkland and he was determined it would go off without a hitch.

Deacon and Julia were coming in on Sunday morning with a busload of kids from the Fallon center in Milton. They were bringing the bags of donated sports equipment to give away. Each bag included a soccer ball, a football, a jump rope, a box of sidewalk chalk and a pair of street-hockey sticks and pucks. They had cases of sneakers and cleats and a group of volunteers organized to help size the kids.

Deacon and Wes had put together a list of playground games they'd run throughout the day. Every kid who came and participated in at least one event got a bag of gear and a pair of sneaks or cleats. Jay had asked why they didn't just give the stuff out, but Deacon was a big believer in investing kids in their own goals. He wanted them to feel as if they'd earned the equipment and that way he hoped they'd feel ownership and maybe get out and use it. He'd also seen enough trouble caused when grown-ups caught the scent of a free deal. Having the kids participate kept the adult interference to a minimum.

His phone rang, interrupting his thoughts.

"Wes," Deacon said. "Everything okay there?"

The false heartiness in his tone made Wes wince. Hell, it probably made Deacon wince. His brother couldn't help it. Deacon had spent so many years worrying about him, being his mother and father, that he couldn't help being protective. Wes had done everything he could to convince his brother he hadn't intentionally flung himself in the path of a beer truck, but the worry lingered like the last sensitive traces of a bruise whose color had faded.

"I'm not playing in traffic, Deacon. Promise."

"Shut up."

"You shut up."

"Did you meet Trish Jones? She give you the check?"

A simple question, but Wes choked on the answer. He wouldn't lie to Deacon, but he wasn't going to accuse Posy or her mom of anything without more evidence.

"Trish is out of town," Wes said. "I met her daughter."

"Did she give you the check?"

"No. She says she has the money, but I haven't seen it yet."

"And you believe her?"

"I believe Posy."

He wasn't so sure about her mom, though. This whole "out of town with a relative" thing was just a bit too pat. That coupled with the fact that Posy hadn't seemed thrilled to meet him and neither of them had turned over the money, he wasn't going to say he was worry free.

"Wes—" Deacon said. But then he stopped.

"What?"

"Nothing. Forget it."

"Deacon, what?"

"No. I promised Julia that I'd back off. You're in charge. If you say things are under control, that's good enough for me."

For God's sake, did Deacon have some psychic pipeline into his brain so he could say the exact thing that made him feel least like he was doing the right thing?

He wanted to believe Posy, but the situation stank. His college roommate once told him he and Deacon had a power differential in their relationship because of the way Deacon saved him when they were kids. He'd said it was an insurmountable debt, and Wes had agreed. Even though he was never going to pay it off, he took every chance he got to chisel away at it.

If there was something going on with this fundraiser that would put the Hand-to-Hand project in danger, then he had to find out about it.

THE DEALER TOOK HIS TIME looking at her mom's stuff. He tried to get her to agree to break up some of the sets, but she refused. He tried harder to make her keep the light-houses and the set of limited-edition Hallmark plates with pictures of state flowers on them, but she stuck to her guidelines. He had to take it all and he had to pay her cash right then.

Four hours later, he and his three sons had packed up every collection. With the money she'd already borrowed from Maddy and her own resources, she was left with a deficit of only eighteen thousand dollars.

She'd just poured herself a celebratory beer when her aunt Phyllis, Maddy's mom, called.

"Maddy told me what your mother did." Her aunt's voice had the same rich tone as Maddy's. "She also told me you're taking out a loan to cover the damages."

"Please keep it a secret." Her aunt was married to her dad's brother. She'd been a voice of reason over the years when Posy felt overwhelmed by her mom. "It would be terrible if anyone found out."

"You mean your mom would be arrested if anyone found out."

"That, too."

"I might have raised a nun," her aunt said, "but I'm no saint."

Posy smiled at the familiar joke.

"I mean that," her aunt continued. "I'm not a saint and I'm not a martyr and this has gone on long enough with your mom, kiddo. Maddy said you swore you'd stop swooping in to rescue Trish if you can get her out of this one last mess."

"Believe me, Aunt Phyllis, it's the truth."

"Then I want to help. How much money do you need?"

Posy was so startled she almost dropped the phone. "No, Aunt Phyllis. You can barely tolerate my mom. I can't let you pay her debts."

"This isn't for Trish. It's for you. My own daughter took a vow of poverty. If I give my money to her order, they'll just use it for more sheep. I want to help you. Right now, while I'm still alive to see you get out from under your mom's crazy."

"I don't even know what to say."

"You can tell me how much you need and then you can say thanks. You can also tell me you'll let me spoil your future children since Maddy, bless her, isn't going to give me any grandchildren."

She thought about lying, giving her aunt a much smaller figure, because she really didn't want to take her money. But then she thought about Wes and the way he looked when he talked about his brother and the Fallon Foundation. She had to make this right and she couldn't let anything, including her pride, get in the way. "Eighteen thousand dollars," she said. "But I'll pay you back as soon as I can. I'm selling my mom's—"

"No explanation necessary. You'll take care of this, Posy. Don't worry about a thing."

After she thanked her aunt so profusely the woman threatened to take her offer back, she hung up the phone. She was so incredibly relieved and upset all at the same time. She was used to cleaning up after her mom, not to asking for help for herself. Shame and relief overwhelmed her. She put her face down on her arms and cried.

Angel came over and put her paws up on her knee. Posy lifted her head and the dog whined. When she picked her up, Angel licked her face once and then leaned against her chest. Posy cried a little more, but somehow holding the dog made her feel less desperate.

When she'd cried herself out, she picked up the phone and called Wes.

WHEN HIS CELL PHONE rang, Wes was asleep on the couch, *SportsCenter* running softly on the TV behind his head. He fumbled in his pocket and pulled the phone out, hoping it wasn't Deacon not so subtly touching base to be sure he hadn't walked in front of another truck.

He didn't recognize the number.

"Hello?"

"Wes, it's Posy Jones. I have your check. Where can I meet you?"

She rushed the entire thing out so fast it took him a second to process what she'd said. When he got it, he stood up and jumped, pumping his fist as if he'd just dunked on a breakaway drive.

"Good," he said into the phone. "That's good."

He hadn't realized how nervous he was about that money until the exhilaration he felt at her call. He was really, really happy that he wasn't going to have to file a police report on Posy's mom.

"Let's go out to—" He almost said "to celebrate," but that would let her know that he'd had his doubts. "I haven't been anywhere in downtown Kirkland yet. I'd love to see the sights."

"I actually have a lot to do here at the house. I'll just meet you somewhere and give you the check. Are you in your office?"

"It's seven o'clock on Saturday night."

And he was asleep on his couch, getting turned down for a date by a very hot woman. Was his life really going to be this pathetic now that he wasn't playing ball? He might as well be at the office.

"Oh, right. So where should we meet?"

"Jay told me about some place called the Lemon Drop Café. Meet me there and I'll buy you a drink." He'd never been a guy who stood on pride when there was the possibility he could talk someone into fun. "Come on, Posy. I'm supposed to be building goodwill for my brother's project but I haven't been anywhere. Where's that small-town hospitality you hear about in the movies?"

"I don't live in Kirkland anymore. Maybe Jay is free."

"He'd probably make me sign his napkin."

He hoped she smiled at that.

"Fine. We can meet at the Lemon Drop. But don't say I didn't warn you."

"Warn me about what?"

"Kirkland is not Madrid."

SHE'D PACKED enough clothes for four days when she came and she was running out of options. She managed to put together a decent outfit, though, pairing her favorite, curve-hugging jeans with a slim tank under a loosely woven silk sweater. The sweater had baggy sleeves that ended at the elbow and a low scoop neck that showed off her collarbone and a touch of cleavage. She rooted through her mom's jewelry box and turned up a pair of dangly silver earrings with small sparkly stones. The outfit was just dressy enough for the Lemon Drop without looking as if she'd put a lot of effort into how she looked.

She clipped Angel's leash on and called the number Maddy had given her for her mom's room at the Knoll. The phone rang while she waited for Angel to do her business in the yard, but when her mom didn't pick up, it transferred over to the Guest Services desk.

She didn't want to leave a message with the person on duty. The fewer people who knew about the money, the better. She hung up and called Maddy.

"The Knoll, Sister Maddy."

She stopped inside the front door to unhook Angel's leash.

"Maddy, it's me." The dog shook herself, collar and tags jingling as her ears flew. Posy slung her purse over her shoulder. "Listen, can you give my mom a message?"

Angel went up the stairs into the living room and Posy took a final look at herself in the mirror in the hall. She finger combed her hair around her shoulders.

"Sure. What's up?"

"Tell her I got the money and everything is taken care of." She opened the front door. "You can also tell her that your mom is my favorite aunt ever and has dibs on my future children for spoiling."

"My mom came through for you?" Maddy asked. "She was pissed when I told her."

"Isn't pissed a little vulgar for a woman of the cloth?"

Holding the cell in one hand, she hitched her bag higher on her shoulder and reached behind her to close the door. Angel scampered out between her feet and shot off around the side of the house.

"Damn it," she said.

"Now who's vulgar?" Maddy asked.

"My mother's dog keeps escaping. Trish better get home quick or I'm putting her schnoodle up for adoption."

"I have to sing in the choir at the evening service or I'd meet you somewhere to celebrate."

"I'm going downtown," Posy said. "With Wes."

Maddy shouted, "Yes!" and Posy held the phone away from her ear.

"Settle down there, Sister Maddy."

"I'm settled. Just have a good time, okay? Your mom is safe with me. The money is in the bank. You're free and clear to enjoy yourself."

She hung up just as an outraged yowl penetrated the night.

A sleek gray cat streaked down her driveway with Angel in hot pursuit.

Enjoy herself. *Right.* She wasn't going to be able to relax until she wrapped up all of her mom's business here in Kirkland.

CHAPTER EIGHT

WES TOOK A QUICK SHOWER and then dressed in dark jeans and a long-sleeve dress shirt. His hair was still too short to need any brushing, so after he rolled his cuffs up and tied his shoes, he was ready to go.

It was early, but he wasn't about to sit in his apartment. He'd already fallen asleep on the couch once and that was more than enough. If he wasn't careful, he'd be keeping the same hours as Mrs. Meacham.

Jay had said the Lemon Drop was right on Main Street, so he walked the five blocks from his apartment to downtown and started south on Main. If he didn't find the café, he'd walk back up the other side of the street.

There was no doubt Kirkland was everything a small town should be. He'd lived in a small town, but Milton was depressed and on the run-down side of shabby. Still, the bars and restaurants that survived in downtown Milton weren't quite as—yuppy?—as the places he was passing now.

A bookstore named Shakespeare's Attic. A yarn store—Crossed Needles. A coffee shop with a chalkboard sign out front advertising iced mocha and homemade blueberry muffins. Every shop he passed looked as if it had come from a movie set or Walt Disney World.

Kirkland wasn't exactly Stepford levels of uncomfortable, but there was something to be said for the tacky honesty of the neon beer signs in the window of the Pond, the thriving pizza place in Milton.

He was almost past the Christmas store when the name painted on the window registered. The Wonders of Christmas Shoppe. Wonders—that was Trish Jones's store. He went back to the door, but the place was locked up and the sign said Closed. He glanced up and down the block. All the other shops and restaurants were open.

He cupped his hands around his eyes and looked through the window, but he couldn't see much more than a cramped, crowded aisle and a bunch of Christmas trees.

For the second time that night, Wes felt an unexpected rush of relief. Her mom really was out of town. He turned away and crossed the street to the café.

SHE SAW HIM as soon as she opened the door at the Lemon Drop. The café tables were mostly small and round, seating four people comfortably and six if they were really good friends. Wes was all alone at a table near the window, his big frame dwarfing the chair. The young guy from the mayor's office was standing next to him.

"Hey," Wes said, raising a hand. "Over here, Posy."

She edged past the two tables between them and then eased her bag down under the table.

"Posy, did you meet Ryan yesterday?"

The guy held his hand out and she shook it. "Nice to see you again, Ryan."

"You, too." He turned back to Wes. "Well, you probably don't want to talk business.... Like I said, I don't think the variance is going to be a problem. The presentation at the zoning hearing will probably be just a formality at this point. I know several of them were donors to the fundraiser Posy's mom ran—Chloe Chastain reached out to a lot of the local businesspeople."

"Perfect. We're announcing the results of the fundraiser at Equipment Day tomorrow."

They chatted for a few more minutes and then Ryan said goodbye.

She picked up a menu and flipped it from front to back. "See anything that looks good?"

"I sure do," Wes said. "Were you fishing for a compliment?"

"No!" Posy said. "I meant the menu."

"Of course you did." He put his menu next to his plate. "I'm having a burger. And you look really nice tonight."

She rolled her eyes. "Do you own the cheesy-pickup-line manual or did you borrow it from some guy on the team?"

"Sincere statements of fact are never cheesy. You do look nice."

The open collar of his shirt emphasized the lean and chiseled lines of his shoulders and neck. A few strands of curly dark hair showed above the unbuttoned second button.

"You look very nice tonight, too," she said. In a world where "very nice" was a synonym for "drop-dead sexy," that was.

He asked questions about Kirkland and she answered as honestly as she could, describing the good and bad of growing up in a small town that prided itself on a reputation for clean and cute. She knew it wasn't universally true, but for her, the daughter of a Main Street shop owner, there'd always been the message that the town was watching. Judging.

On the other hand, the more he told her about the Hand-to-Hand project, the more certain she was that it was a great fit for Kirkland. People were generous here with time and money and his program offered a breadth of interests that would draw volunteers, she was sure.

They'd each had a piece of pie and as they were waiting for the waitress to bring the bill, Posy pulled out her purse. She opened the zippered inside pocket where she kept her emergency cash and pulled out the check she'd written to the Fallon Foundation.

Her hand shook, bumping against his as she handed it over. "Sorry," she said. "I never wrote a check that big before." She felt sick to her stomach, looking at her signature, but she wasn't sure if that was from relief or worry. She couldn't believe she'd just written a check to a charity for an amount that was very close to her annual salary. She hoped her mom's house would sell quickly and that she'd be able to pay her aunt and her cousin back.

Wes held the check. "I'm still floored that a simple blog posting could pull in this kind of money."

Posy realized a woman had stopped next to their table and she looked up.

Chloe Chastain. Of all the rotten, rotten luck.

"Posy," Chloe said. "What a surprise. When your mom left town suddenly, I assumed she was visiting you."

"She's actually on a silent retreat out at the Knoll."

"A silent retreat," Chloe said. "Trish?"

Chloe had always been pretty, with big blue eyes and blond hair. Her hair wasn't naturally blond anymore, but highlights had been expertly applied to give her warm brown hair a fresh boost. She'd changed in other ways, too, but there wasn't a single thing Posy could put her finger on. She'd subtly grown from a pretty but mean-spirited girl into a woman who looked calculated—too carefully put together, but still undeniably gorgeous.

Everything she said had an undercurrent, though. Or at least Posy thought it did.

Chloe smiled at Wes.

"Chloe Chastain." She held out her hand. "Are you new in town or just visiting like Posy?"

Wes pushed his chair back and stood in one fluid motion. He took Chloe's hand and shook it warmly.

"Chloe Chastain!" he said. "I'm Wes Fallon. I was so sorry I couldn't connect with you yesterday. My family can't thank you enough for the help you gave with the fundraiser. It was flat-out fantastic."

Chloe pressed his hand between both of hers. "When

I heard about the good work your foundation does, I couldn't help myself. But it was really my readers…and Trish's, of course…who did the hard work."

She held on to Wes's hand as she looked back at Posy. "Your mom went on a retreat, you said? Is that why I haven't been able to get in touch with her since she collected the money?"

"I gave the check to Wes a few minutes ago, so everything is all set." She pointed to it on the table. A moment ago she'd felt sick, but now she felt a twinge of pride. Her mom had made a big mistake, but she'd fixed it so now there was no way Chloe could get to Trish.

Chloe smiled and cocked her head toward the check. "I'm still shocked by how much my readers contributed. It's an impressive number, isn't it?" Then her eyebrows drew together and she looked more closely. "Why is it written on your account, Posy? I thought your mom had a special account set up for the money from donors?"

Damn it. Why hadn't she asked her mom about that? "She's on retreat," Posy repeated helplessly.

Wes picked the check up and looked at it more closely, but when Chloe edged toward it, he folded it and slid it into the chest pocket of his shirt.

"Well, I don't see how you could write it from your account—" Chloe started.

"It's nothing for you to worry about, Chloe. I gave Wes all the documentation for the donors. He has the check. Everything's settled."

"We'll see you at the ceremony at Equipment Day tomorrow," Wes said. "My brother and sister-in-law want to thank you in person."

Chloe pushed her bracelets up her arm and nodded. "I'll be there. Wouldn't miss it. I can't wait to see Trish again."

Posy excused herself to use the restroom and when she came back out, Chloe and Wes were both gone. For a moment she thought they'd left together, maybe to head straight to police headquarters. But then she saw Wes pacing outside, his long-legged stride in fitted jeans sexier than normal for Main Street in Kirkland.

"THAT'S YOUR MOM'S STORE across the street?" he asked when she joined him outside.

Posy nodded. "Wonders. That's it."

"Can we go in?"

"You want to shop?"

What he wanted was to spend some more time with Posy to figure out what the hell was going on. Chloe had hinted that he should look more closely at the finances for the fundraiser and that she would be doing her own digging. He had to admit, it didn't look quite right that the check had come from Posy's personal account. But the point was that the money was there and the donors would get their acknowledgments that their funds were received.

He still felt a nagging worry, though. Getting the money wasn't the only point.

If Chloe decided to stir up trouble for Trish, she'd be

stirring up trouble for Deacon, as well. He hoped she was just talking, but he wasn't sure.

"I'd like to see it. Your mom ran this fundraiser for us on her store blog—it's part of the Fallon Foundation lore now."

"Wonders is part of your lore," Posy said. "I don't even know how to respond to that."

They crossed the street together and she dug a set of keys out of her huge bag. When she opened the door, a set of bells jingled and a wave of holiday-scented air hit him.

"Sorry. The place has been closed up for a few days."

She stepped inside and flicked on a few panels of lights while he took in the space.

"Holy cow, Posy. There is a lot of stuff here."

She moved behind him and closed and locked the door again.

"The Wonders of Christmas. All here at your fingertips."

It was impossible to take the place in all at once. He was astounded at the sheer number of things her mom had for sale. And many of them were very detailed. He leaned down to inspect a tiny village scene with skaters on a pond and a chapel with a flock of pigeons around the steps. Each pigeon was the size of a raisin. He picked one up and looked at the price tag. Two bucks a bird. The flock would cost as much as a ticket to see his old team play in Madrid.

"People pay for this stuff?"

"Not enough," Posy said. "The store's been losing

money. That's why it's closed. My mom's going out of business."

He started to walk toward the front of the store, but he ran into a garland someone had strung at strangulation level right across the aisle.

"Sorry about that," Posy said.

He ducked and carefully extricated himself. "My fault."

She stayed near the door while he made his way toward the register. He stopped near a manger scene that was at once realistic and spiritual. The faces of the figures were painted in a way that reflected their humanity, with care lines and even laugh wrinkles near their eyes.

"This is amazing, Posy." He bent over so he could see the figures more clearly. Even the stable was nicely detailed. He lifted a camel and touched the tassel on its head collar. "My sister-in-law would love this. Can I buy one?"

Posy threw her head back. "You're shopping?"

He put the camel down and picked up a king. "I guess so."

She came up and stood near him, the lights from outside pooling on the floor of the store near them, but leaving her in the shadows thrown by the dim lights she'd turned on inside the store. "Seriously?"

He put the king down, being careful to put it in the exact spot he'd found it. "I can come back some other time if you don't want to pack it up now."

She lifted her arms and let them fall in a gesture of surrender. "I'll go in the back and find a box. I have to get rid of all this stuff for my mom anyway, so I'm not going to turn down a customer."

He followed her into the stockroom at the back of the store. "You're helping your mom close the store?"

"Not so much helping as doing the whole thing for her."

"Why?"

"It's just how things go with my mom. She is... easily overwhelmed." Posy sounded resigned and maybe slightly bitter, but not angry. "I've been bugging her to close the store and sell her house for years. Now that she's actually willing to do it, I don't mind taking care of things for her. It's how our relationship works."

He remembered Chloe's face when she saw Posy's signature on the check. He didn't want to think about what other things Posy might have taken care of for her mother.

"What's she going to do once all this is gone?"

"I'm not sure. She has a boyfriend. Or maybe she'll get an apartment here."

"And you'll be there to help her figure it all out?"

"No. She's going to figure it out on her own this time."

He started to laugh, but she said, "Nope. I'm really finished. I love her, but she's got to start handling her own life."

That wasn't what he'd expected to hear. Was Posy really going to cut her mom off? Could she? He knew families were all different. He'd lived with enough bad examples to know exactly how wrong families could get their relationships. He just hadn't expected to hear Posy say something like that.

When they got back to the manger display with a box and a stack of tissue paper, Wes started to help her wrap the pieces and stow them.

"You must have had the most amazing Christmases when you were a kid," he said.

She wrinkled her nose. "My mom's a Christmas professional. That translates into a lot of stress about details and schedules that are way, way too busy. When my parents were together, they fought almost every year for the entire month of December. After they divorced, I'd go to my dad's the day after Christmas and stay through New Year's. He had an artificial tree and a stocking for me and we'd get a tray of cookies from the bakery down the street."

"I spent Christmas in the police station when I was five," he said. "That one was certainly a highlight."

He didn't know why he blurted that out, but when she suddenly laughed, putting down the king she'd been wrapping to cover her mouth, he was glad he did.

"What happened?"

And then he had to tell her.

Of course he had to tell her. He'd set himself up and there was no way out. He must have subconsciously done it on purpose. He never told these stories, but for some reason, he wanted to tell Posy.

"My brother is ten years older than me. When our parents died, we got split up in foster care. I was…" He never knew how to explain what he'd been like back then. He had nightmares every once in a while in which he was running through a house opening doors and looking for Deacon. That was probably how he'd felt when he was little, but he didn't remember. Not really. "A handful. Wild, I guess. I ran away a lot, looking for Deacon mostly."

He pushed the figure he'd wrapped down into the box. She'd stopped working, but he kept going, not wanting to give the story more importance than it deserved.

"Anyway, I ran away on Christmas and after they found me, Deacon and I spent the day at the police station. The cops bought us dinner out of the vending machine."

"Why?"

"Why what?"

"Why did you spend the day at the police station? Didn't your foster parents come to get you?"

"Social services was waiting for an emergency placement so they could move me. That particular foster mother had had enough, I guess." He tried to make it a joke, but when he made the mistake of glancing at Posy, she had one hand over her mouth.

"She'd had enough of you on Christmas?"

"Maybe she thought I started it," he said. "I did run away."

"Don't," Posy said. "You don't have to make it funny."

He made himself stop talking, but if he couldn't make the moment funny, couldn't brush it aside, then what was left? Him and Posy and this connection between them. She must have felt it, too.

She put her hands on his shoulders and stretched up to kiss him. "I don't need you to make it funny," she whispered against his lips, her kiss hesitant, but sweet.

He savored her lips on his. He'd been wanting to kiss her, wanting to touch her. He rested his hands on her hips lightly, because she seemed to be unsure.

He deepened the kiss and she leaned into him. He pulled back, resting his forehead on hers. This was nothing like their first encounter on the basketball court. He was vulnerable now in a different way, letting her see not just under his surface, but all the way to the core where he still carried some of the kid who'd been tossed out so many times.

He wanted her to understand where he was coming from so she'd know why he had to care about the details of the fundraiser. It wasn't about her mom. It was about him and Deacon.

"That's why the foundation matters more than anything to me, Posy. Why I can't let Deacon down." He paused. He wanted to say this so she'd understand. "He was the only person who cared about me. He did everything he knew…more than you'd believe a kid could… to get me out of foster care. When he signed his NBA contract, I was eight and he took me to live with him. We never had Christmas like this." He gestured around the store. "He was eighteen years old and trying to do a man's job and raise me at the same time. So our life wasn't what you'd see on a postcard for a place like Kirkland. But he saved me. He wants me to do this job for him now and I can't let him down."

Mary was the last figure left in the manger. He picked the piece up and wrapped it carefully.

Posy watched him until the figure was settled in the box. "I get it. I do."

IN SOME WAYS they were so much alike. Both of them were making choices based on the things someone they loved needed from them.

But she was getting out. Once she closed the store and sold her mom's house, she wasn't going to pick up the pieces for Trish anymore.

Seeing Wes's face when he talked about his brother showed her that if Deacon wanted something or needed something, Wes was going to be there for him. Always.

That might be right for them, but it wasn't right for her, not anymore.

"What about when you're finished with this contract for Deacon? Do you have plans?"

He shook his head. "Not yet."

"You deserve plans of your own."

"Is that what you're doing?" he asked. "Selling your mom's store and helping her downsize? Is that for her or for you?"

"It's for both of us, I guess," Posy said. "She's not like your brother, Wes. I can't expect you to understand how I feel."

She tucked the flaps of the box in and closed it. "I hope your sister-in-law likes this," she said. "I'll dig out the certificate that goes with it and get it to you. They're all one of a kind. It's a nice gift. You're a very nice guy."

She said it as if it was goodbye. She didn't want to say goodbye, so why had she? Because she needed to learn to stand on her own, to stand up for herself and to keep her mom out of her life. If she got involved with Wes, she'd just be trading one overly dependent family dynamic for another. Until Wes grew up enough to have his own life, he was going to be jumping to do what his brother wanted. How would she have the strength to hold firm against her mom's needs if she was with someone who put family above everything else? She couldn't do it. No matter how he made her feel.

They walked back through the store together. When she came to the garland he'd tangled with, she gave it a sharp yank. The whole thing came down, knocking a row of miniature Christmas trees off the shelf.

He turned back to help her pick them up, but she stepped over them. "Just leave it. I have to come in and start clearing things out next week."

He held the box as she locked the door and then the two of them stood awkwardly on the sidewalk under a streetlight.

"I don't think I'm going to come to the event tomorrow, Wes. I have a lot of projects to complete and you're going to be busy with your family."

"Posy, please come. I want Deacon and my sister-in-law to meet you," he said. "I want to spend more time with you."

She made the mistake of looking at him. His eyes were shining in the dark. She remembered the way he'd looked when they'd played basketball the other day—

how free and fierce he'd been then and how much she'd loved meeting him step for step. Maybe that guy was in there somewhere, under the obligations he felt toward his brother and all the other baggage.

She decided it was worth the chance.

"Okay."

He shifted the box to the side and kissed her again. She closed her eyes. His kisses were firm and gentle, with an undercurrent of longing that made her want to take more from him. She leaned against him for a second, brushing the tips of her breasts against the hard muscle of his chest and letting one thigh slide between his.

The box poked her in the side and she remembered where they were—smack in the middle of Main Street, outside the store. She pulled back.

"I'll see you tomorrow," she promised.

When she walked back toward her car, she saw Chloe walking up the other side of the street with her sister, Felicity. They didn't wave, but Chloe definitely saw her, because she made eye contact and smiled.

Had she seen the kiss?

What did that smile mean?

CHAPTER NINE

ON SUNDAY, WES GOT TO the Kirkland Community Center where they were hosting Equipment Day more than an hour before his brother's bus with the kids from Milton was supposed to arrive. He had the schedule planned in fifteen-minute intervals and had triple-checked everything from the lists of kids who'd been preregistered either through the Kirkland center or through a human services agency in the county. The refreshments had been delivered and were being organized in the tent outside by the group of volunteers Ryan and Jay had rounded up.

He was impatient now for Deacon to get here so he could get the day rolling. He wondered if Posy was going to show. She'd like Deacon and Julia. He hoped she was coming.

Last night had been odd. He was definitely attracted to her. He liked the way she met him head-on and asked him questions that made him think. And feel.

He'd also been uncomfortable with the way she was disposing of her mom's belongings and seemed adamant that she was going to check out of the woman's life. But then he didn't know them very well. He wanted to believe Posy was better than that. He wanted to believe she was someone who'd stay true to the people in her life. That mattered.

A truck was just pulling away, leaving a stack of root-beer kegs on the lawn. Wes practically jumped at the chance to wrestle the kegs around to the back of the re-freshment tent where bags of ice were lined up to keep them cold throughout the day.

The Milton bus still hadn't arrived when he was fin-ished with the kegs. He made one last circuit of the field, checking the setup for the foul-shooting contest and the soccer-kick net. Jay had a buddy who worked at the university, and the athletics department had lent them a batting cage and radar gun they could use to clock pitching speeds.

While he was making a loop around the parking lot to check on the signs they'd put up, Posy's Jeep pulled in. He jogged over to her. Music was pumping from the speakers and Posy was flipping her head up and down, dancing in her seat to the last notes. She stopped danc-ing when she saw him, but didn't turn the radio off until the song ended.

"Kelly Clarkson, huh?"

"That's right." Her skin was the perfect golden-brown other women spent money on in tanning booths. Her cheeks were pink and he wondered if the blush was caused by embarrassment because he'd caught her danc-ing or just from the exercise.

When they'd played basketball, her skin had been flushed that day, too.

Today she had on a slim-cut T-shirt and a pair of navy

track pants. His ex, Fabi, had always told him she would never be caught dead in public in sweatpants, but Wes thought Posy looked good.

"You're going to like my brother," he said.

Posy crossed her arms. "I'm kind of uncomfortable being part of the ceremony. My mom did all the work for this. Maybe it would be better if you just made your announcement and left me out of it."

He laughed. "No way. The crowd is going to want to thank you personally." She ducked her head, looking away from him.

He'd gotten an email from Chloe last night. It was cheerful and included quite a few exclamation points, but she mentioned that she was going to pop into the bank on Monday just to be sure everything with the fundraiser account was taken care of.

It had planted another seed of doubt about Posy's mom. Knowing that was probably exactly what Chloe wanted didn't make it any easier to ignore his suspicions.

Growing up the way he did, bounced from home to home, with adults constantly making decisions about him, he'd been on edge almost all the time. Unfortunately for him and his foster parents, his anxiety and fear had manifested as aggressive, irresponsible acting out. Now Wes made a conscious effort to avoid people and situations he couldn't be sure of. "Listen," he said to Posy, "I'm sorry if I was badgering you about the money. It's just something I needed to check off my list. We're all set now, right?"

"Absolutely," she replied. "Nothing to worry about."

A loud horn sounded from the street and he turned to see the Milton bus pulling in.

"All right. Time to get this day started. Let's go meet Deacon and Julia."

"I'm really not sure I should stay."

"Why not? Posy, you have to be here." He pointed toward the field behind the center. "How else am I going to be able to beat you at the free-throw contest?"

OF COURSE HE MENTIONED basketball.

And they'd kissed last night. Twice.

She'd thought about their basketball game quite a bit last night in bed.

"Come on, Posy," he said. "You don't want my brother to think Jay is my only Kirkland friend, do you?"

"Fine," she said.

"Can you do me a favor?" he asked. "I meant to grab a folder from my desk and I forgot. It's right on top and it's labeled Volunteers. You remember where my office is, right?"

She nodded.

He jogged away across the parking lot and she gave herself a second to admire the back view of Wes Fallon. His black golf shirt was tugged tight across his shoulders, and his legs in dark jeans were very long. In college, she'd dated a guy from the wrestling team. He'd been rock-hard, solid muscle from his scalp to his feet. If she'd been a sculptor, she could have used him for inspiration for a piece called *War* or *Power*. Sculpting solid rock was one thing, sleeping with it was something entirely different and she hadn't liked it much. His proportions had been all wrong and his neck was as thick as one of her thighs.

She much preferred Wes's athletic grace. He wasn't weak and he certainly wasn't soft, but she imagined in bed his chest would be the perfect place to rest her head and his arms around her would feel strong, but not confining.

Some kids were playing knee hockey in the lobby of the building, scrambling on all fours, clutching the short sticks one-handed. She slid along the edge of the game and found Wes's office door open.

He'd decorated somewhat, she noticed. A picture of him with an older guy and smiling woman sat on the desk. His brother and sister-in-law no doubt. There was another photo of Wes in a basketball uniform with his arm around the same older guy—it had to be Deacon. Wes looked young, maybe it was from college. His hair was so long, she was surprised to see how different he looked with the edges softening the lines of his face.

She saw the folder on top of a stack of forms in the middle of his desk. She turned to leave, but couldn't quite make herself go out the door.

She'd paid the money back. But she worried anyway. Chloe's smile had been on her mind. Seeing how excited he was about this center and bringing his brother's work to Kirkland made her realize that she really didn't have any business being with him. Every step he took to solidify the relationship with his foundation and Kirkland would be undone if Chloe found out her mom stole the money.

She wished she were a different person or that her relationship with her mom had been different. With a last look around, she closed the office door and went back outside.

IN THE PARKING LOT a mass of middle school and high school–age kids were clustered around Wes and a few other adults. One she knew was his brother, and the woman standing between them must be his sister-in-law. The other two guys were younger and looked like brothers.

"Posy!" Wes called. He waved her over. "This is my brother, Deacon, and his wife, Julia. Posy Jones—the daughter of our fundraising champion. And these guys are Trey and Shawn Baez. They're finishing up high school in Milton—Trey's graduating this year—and they coach the peewee basketball team at the Fallon center."

She shook hands all around. Deacon wasn't as tall as Wes and his hair was lighter, dark blond as opposed to Wes's black, but their matching deep blue eyes marked them as brothers. Julia, who looked a little older than Deacon, reached to shake hands as she said, "Wes told us you welcomed him to town. Thanks for everything you're doing."

Deacon shook her hand, as well. "We owe your mom a huge thank-you."

Posy just nodded.

Wes flung an arm around Trey's shoulders. "Trey and Shawn inspired the Fallon centers." He turned over the name tag the younger man was wearing on a lanyard around his neck and pointed to the Fallon center logo, a silhouette of a young boy on a man's shoulder's shooting a basket. "That's Shawn right there."

Shawn smirked. "They picked me because I'm the good-looking one."

"They picked you because I was grounded the day the guy came to take the pictures," Trey said. "Your buzz is growing out, Wes. Want me to shave it again?"

Wes rubbed the back of his head. "No, sir. It can't grow back fast enough for me."

Deacon said, "You used to beg me to let you buzz your hair when you were little."

"And then I grew up and realized how awful you looked when you buzzed yours."

Shawn whistled, a sharp sound that caught the attention of two boys who were horsing around near the curb. "Knock it off!" he called. "We better get them moving before they're run over."

Trey and Shawn helped to sort the Milton kids into groups to unload the equipment from the back of the van behind the bus. Julia and Deacon headed off to find Jay to discuss plans with him. She and Wes were left standing next to the bus.

"That's a neat story about Shawn and the logo."

"Yeah. Deacon and I coached the girls basketball team in Milton about ten years ago. Those guys hung around every day because their sister was on the team and there was no one at home to watch them."

"You and your brother went back to Milton?"

He lifted his chin and then sighed. "It's a long story and we have to get this day started."

She looked out toward the back of the center where colorful flags fluttered on the refreshment tent and the shrill voices of excited kids were blending with the music just starting to pump through the outdoor sound system. She'd been at events like this every weekend of her childhood.

Wes was looking forward to it and all she could think about was how many times she was going to have to fudge the truth about her mom and the donations. She reminded herself this was the last time.

She followed Wes as he waded into the day, but then as she watched him interact with the kids and adults, volunteers and attendees, she realized he was coming at this from a different place than she'd expected. When her mom volunteered, she made sure everyone around her knew how hard she was working and how hectic her life was. She was a martyr to her volunteer commitments and she wanted people to know it.

Wes threw all his energy into this day, but not because he wanted to be noticed. He wanted the event to be a success. He spent more time watching his brother than anything else.

The stations where the young athletes were competing to earn their equipment bags had been carefully planned to spark wide interest. Wes and Posy worked their way through the stops, making sure to test each of the choices.

She thought he was joking when he said the first thing he wanted to test was the cotton-candy machine, but she went along with him and then watched as he ate a huge swirl of blue fluff. When he was finished, they headed for the soccer-kick station.

The kids needed to move through at least five of the stations and get a stamp on their card before they could earn an equipment bag. They didn't need to win the games at the stations, just take a turn, but when they got to the soccer-kick station, a small girl with two missing front teeth was practically in tears. She wanted to score on the goalie before she got the stamp on her card, but all her shots had been blocked.

The kids behind her in line were starting to get impatient and one of them called out that she should give it up and let someone else have a turn. Posy knew exactly how the girl felt. She didn't like to be handed things she hadn't earned and participation wasn't a high enough bar. The girl had blond hair pulled back in a ponytail and her fists were clamped tight around the hem of her T-shirt.

"My turn isn't over until I score," she insisted to the bigger boy who was running the station.

"You get three kicks, Mary, and that's it."

"I want to score."

Two boys standing in line rolled their eyes and Mary saw them. She gave her ponytail a flick and stood her ground. Wes stepped between the two of them. "Mary, there's a line behind you waiting for a turn."

"But I want to score."

"Who wouldn't?" he said.

Posy broke in, "I'll take a turn in goal. If you don't make it on this kick, then you have to let the other kids have a turn."

"You're going to let it go in on purpose," she said.

"Let it in on purpose?" she said, her eyes wide. "I will do no such thing."

She walked over and switched places with the boy who'd been guarding the net. She got into a goalie stance, bent knees, weight on the balls of her feet, arms spread wide. "Go!"

Mary took a running start and gave the ball a big boot. It sailed toward the goal, straight and true.

Posy counted off three breaths before she dived for the ball, which dropped behind her as she landed on her knees in the grass. Mary tilted her head, not sure if she was being babied.

"You were late," Wes said to Posy. He took the girl's card and stamped it, saying, "Good kick."

She seemed satisfied with his matter-of-fact assessment because she stuck her tongue out at the boys behind her before she ran off. Posy rubbed at a stain on her knee as she came out of the goal.

Walking toward the basketball court with Wes, she said, "Sorry for butting in. She was being a brat."

"It didn't matter if she got the goal. She could have gotten her card stamped anyway."

She didn't have an answer for that. Didn't feel like telling him she'd seen herself in a bratty kid who wanted to win more than she wanted to be liked.

"Did you let it in on purpose?"

"She's eight years old."

"So, yes?" Wes raised an eyebrow.

"God, Wes," Posy said. "Why does it matter?"

"It doesn't matter to me," he answered. "But you stepped in as if it mattered to you."

After checking on the basketball games, they stopped by the prize table where kids who'd completed their cards were picking up their equipment bags. Lined up about seven deep, they were getting antsy, so Wes and Posy went around to help check some of them out. The holdup was getting their feet sized for shoes, so they grabbed a folding chair and one of the templates to measure the kids' feet and settled in.

The first few went pretty quickly. One boy was bothered that they only had blue or red stripes on the sneakers because his favorite color was green, but he cheered up when Posy swapped the soccer ball in his bag for one with green markings.

The next kid who sat in her chair looked a little like what Wes might have looked like when he was a kid. He wore a Yankees cap with a frayed brim turned backward on his head and thick black hair stuck out over his ears and at the back of his neck.

"This sucks," he muttered. He swung his foot and it might have been just an innocent fidget or it might have been a half-serious attempt to kick her. She was about to tell him to cool down when she realized he was doing his best not to cry, but it wasn't working very well. A tear dropped and he used the back of his hand to smear it quickly away. "I hate this place."

He toed his sneaker off and stood to put his foot in the template to be measured. "Stupid people with stupid rules."

Wes knelt next to the boy's leg and fiddled with the template. "Size five."

"We have red or blue stripes. Which one do you want?" Posy said.

"Blue." He crossed his arms and sat back in the chair. "This sucks," he repeated.

Posy looked for the right size in the stacks of boxes while Wes said, "Okay, buddy, what's bothering you?"

She handed the box to Wes and then crouched next to him.

"That lady over there is stupid," he said. "All I wanted was an extra bag for my brother because he couldn't come today because he has detention at school. And even though he was *supposed* to come and even though he was *planning* to be here and even though the detention was not his fault because he only hit Josh *after* Josh hit him, they said I can't have a bag for him because you have to be here in person to get one." He swiped at another tear angrily. "I am not crying." He glared at them as if daring them to challenge that statement. "I'm mad because I promised my brother and this place sucks."

The last word came with a sound that might have

been a sob and he turned his hat around and pulled the brim over his face. His shoulders shook but he didn't make a sound.

"Sit tight for a second," Wes said and then he mouthed to Posy, "Watch him."

He walked over to the woman with the clipboard who was overseeing the bag giveaway. The kid's face was still covered, but Posy whispered to him, "He's going to take care of this. Don't worry." Being the rich guy in charge of the foundation came in handy when it was time to break the rules. She looked back again, but the woman and Wes were still talking, so she touched the kid's knee and added, "Want me to help you put your new shoes on? You can wear them home."

He didn't seem to have heard her, but then he toed off his other sneaker and stuck his foot out toward her. She barely heard him say, "Yes, please."

The soft "please" was the part that made her cry, but luckily the kid kept his hat pulled down. She slid the new sneakers on over his dirty socks and was tying the second knot when Wes dropped a bag on the ground next to the chair. At the sound, the boy's head came up so fast it was almost comical.

Wes crouched again and said, "Here's a bag for your brother." He kept his hand on the bag while he continued. "I give you credit for keeping your promise to him and looking out for him, but next time, try to keep your temper, all right? No kicking and don't call people stupid. Everybody here is doing their best, so we all have to stay calm."

The boy nodded.

"Have fun, then."

"Thanks!"

Posy smiled at the transformation in the boy's expression. Every bit of the sullen temper was gone, replaced by a sparkling grin.

After he was gone, she said to Wes, "You made his day."

"We have extra bags."

She nodded toward the lady with the clipboard. "What did she say to you?"

"Just that we made the rule so the kids wouldn't take extras to sell. I guess they did a giveaway like this one time and then the equipment ended up on Craigslist. She questioned if he even had a brother."

"What did you tell her?"

"What if he does?"

She realized then that what she'd seen as a generically kind gesture, the kind of thing anyone would have done for the boy who'd been so obviously heartsick over his brother, hadn't been random for Wes. He hadn't given the kid a bag because it was easy or because they had extras or because he'd felt sorry for him. He'd seen himself and his brother in the situation. His connection to Deacon was always on his mind.

Motivating his every action.

WES WAS HAVING a great time. He wouldn't admit it to Deacon, but he'd been a little bored the past few days. Not that he didn't think the work the center was doing was amazing and not that he didn't want to be involved. He did.

It was just… He'd spent most of the past ten years playing competitive sports. Switching to this suburban, nine-to-five lifestyle was a shock to his system. He loved helping Mrs. M. with her weeding. And Posy was keeping him on his toes. But he missed the hard bite of competition. He missed being able to throw everything he had into a game and know the guys he was playing with were giving everything they had right back.

He hadn't felt that energy since he left Madrid. Except for that one basketball game with Posy.

He glanced around, but didn't see her. She'd told him she was going for a bottle of water, so he assumed she'd be back soon. In the meantime, he had to do something with the bigger boys. With less than an hour left, most of the kids had tried the events they were interested in. Some of the older boys had started milling around, chasing each other, and generally drifting toward mayhem.

Wes could relate. He was wound up and ready to kick the games up a notch.

A teenager dodged past him, holding a baseball cap that must have belonged to one of the other three boys racing behind him. Wes snagged the kid in the lead and held him by the arm.

"That your hat?"

The kid stuck it on his head. "Yes, sir."

Wes straightened up and gave the kid a look that made him take the hat off and toss it sullenly to one of the other boys.

"Okay, all you guys come with me."

He kept his hold on the kid's arm, so it wasn't much of a choice. Trey and Shawn were bagging recyclables at the refreshment tent and he hollered for them when he went past.

The Wiffle ball station was at the far end of the soccer field and it hadn't seen as much traffic during the day as the other ones. Wes had collected a group of about ten of the bigger kids plus Trey and Shawn by the time he reached the piece of carpet that was serving as a batter's box. Posy arrived just as he was explaining the rules to the kids.

"Three of you get in the outfield. The rest of you line up here to hit. You get three pitches and have to hit one or you're out. You get out, you cycle out and field for the other guys. Once we're down to three people, we're going for distance. I'll pitch."

Wes picked up a bucket full of Wiffle balls. The guys were lining up, shoving each other to determine who had to field first. Shawn snatched a bat and called dibs on first bats.

He jogged out to the sweatshirt they'd been using to mark the pitcher's mound. With two balls in his hands, he straightened to face Shawn only to find that Posy had somehow gotten first at bat.

CHAPTER TEN

THE OLD COMPETITIVE ENERGY had started flowing the second he'd caught that hat thief, but now, facing Posy again, he was surprised by a surge of excitement. Now things were getting interesting.

"They used to call me Smoke back at my old elementary school," he said.

She pressed her lips closed to hold back her smile, but he saw the dimple flash in her cheek that gave her away.

"I had a kitten named Smoke one time. Cute little thing. I used to tickle its stomach and it would just roll right over."

"Here, kitty," Shawn called. Wes glared at him, but Shawn only laughed. "Pitch the ball, old man."

He got set to throw, staring down Posy who was in a textbook-perfect crouch at the plate. Holding the bat angled behind her head. Knees bent. Butt out. He released the ball late and it wafted toward the plate with about eighty percent less speed than he'd planned. She crushed it, of course.

As she handed the bat to the hat thief, he thought he heard her snicker, "Smoke."

He struck out a couple and two of them hung on by the skin of their teeth, snicking a piece of the ball, just enough to pop it up back to him. Two girls had jumped in line after they saw Posy batting and they both got a piece of the ball.

At the end of the first round eight batters were left in the game.

"I'm through going easy on you," Wes yelled as he loaded his pockets with spare balls. "This was fun while it lasted, but I've got other places to be."

More people had drifted over to watch, including some of the adults who'd been running the ticket stand and the refreshment table. He saw Chloe Chastain and a woman who looked enough like her that she had to be her sister. Chloe waved to him and he waved back.

Posy was up first again. "Less talk and more throwing, Smoke."

He held the ball, staring her down, partly to entertain the kids who were watching and partly because it was a great excuse to stare at Posy. She was clearly enjoying herself, but he could see just as clearly that she was poised and ready to swing. In the moment before he threw, the joking fell away and the competition held her focus, the same way it held his.

He stretched through the end of the throw, putting his muscles into it, and sending it straight and hard right down the middle.

Posy didn't flinch. Her bat came through and launched the ball into the outfield. She watched it go with a satisfied smile.

Wes put his hands on his hips. "Next one's not going to be a cantaloupe right down the middle like that one."

Shawn took her place. "You keep throwing her those easy ones and she's going to win the whole thing."

Posy jabbed him with her bat and he danced out of her way.

He got four of the kids out, including one of the girls. Then Trey was at the plate.

He went through an elaborate routine, kicking the grass, tapping his bat, pulling on the brim of his cap. Then he got in the batter's box in his crouch, but looked over his shoulder back toward Posy. "You want me to hit it to right field or left?"

Wes beaned him.

Hey, it was only a Wiffle ball and a guy couldn't be expected to take insults all day. Trey pretended to charge the mound and Shawn pretended to have to subdue him. The kid who'd stolen the hat fell over he was laughing so hard.

Wes looked for Posy and she brushed her index fingers together, tsking him.

Trey went back to the plate, but he whiffed all three pitches.

"Can't expect a man to bat when he's got a concussion," he complained as he flung the bat down in disgust. "I'm sending a protest to the commissioner."

That left them with three batters in the game, Posy, Shawn and the other girl.

"All right," he said. "Whoever hits it the farthest in this round is the winner. You can take all three of your pitches and we'll count the farthest shot." He turned to wave the kids in from the outfield. "Don't pick these up until they're all finished."

Shawn went up to the plate first.

Wes called time-out and pointed to a couple of little girls sitting on the ground on the sidelines halfway between the plate and his pitcher's mound. "Be careful there, kids. You're sitting right where his ball is going to come down."

Shawn hit the first ball right back at him and he had to jump to avoid getting hit in the leg.

Wes shook his head. "It's not a good idea to antagonize Smoke."

Shawn missed the next pitch and then hit the third one straight out, over Wes's head into the outfield.

He was pretty sure he'd just seen the game winner, but he put three nice ones over the plate for the other girl. She got a piece of all of them, but really ripped the last one. It was a nice hit, but fell short of Shawn's ball.

He watched it land and then spun back, ready to pitch to Posy. She'd taken off her track pants and was at the plate in a pair of short knit shorts. He dropped the ball he was holding. Her legs were amazing. Toned, tanned and miles long. He glanced around. Almost everyone who'd been at the event was gathered around watching. He saw Deacon standing behind Julia with his arms folded around her. Wes had been there, coaching with them, during the season when they fell in love. Was this what it felt like when you found your life constantly turned upside down?

He faced the plate again. Posy settled into her stance,

which meant she wiggled her butt and dug one sneaker into the dirt, lengthening the muscle in her calf and totally destroying his focus on the ball.

His first pitch bounced in the dirt three feet in front of the plate.

"Tired?" she asked.

"You want a younger arm in there, Wes?" Trey added.

For his second throw, he looked her right in the eye. He wound up and threw, not sure where the ball would go, but never once breaking eye contact with her. She took a cut at it, but it was inside and popped up right back to him.

Okay. Now he knew he wasn't the only one feeling whatever this thing was between them.

This time he gave her a real pitch. He focused, bore down and sent it blazing toward the plate. She caught it cleanly and it rocketed past him into the outfield, dropping down a few feet past Shawn's ball.

She lifted the bat in triumph while Shawn and Trey and the other kids swarmed her.

He was going to congratulate her and offer her a special prize, but she was in a crowd, so he detoured to the sidelines to pick up a few stray balls.

Chloe and her friend were talking to Jay. He came up on them in time to hear her say, "That's exactly why no one ever liked her."

"Come on, it was just a game," Jay protested.

"It wasn't a game to her, though. You saw how she gets. All those kids out there and she had to be the winner."

Wes glanced back toward Posy, but she was much too far away to hear. The players were still gathered around her and Trey and Shawn were obviously replaying the best moments from the game. None of them looked particularly injured that Posy had beaten them. It wasn't as if any of them were little kids—he thought they'd all been high schoolers. It certainly hadn't occurred to him or Trey or Shawn to let one of the kids win.

"She's just so intense," Chloe said. "When we were young, her mom always told my mom she's too much. You've been spending a lot of time with her, Wes. What do you think?"

"I think Julia's going to be mad if I don't get up there and help them get this thank-you ceremony started. You're our guest of honor, Chloe. You don't want to be late."

Wes grabbed the last ball and turned his back on them, but he could feel her eyes on him. He wasn't sure why she hated Posy so much, but it made him nervous.

He didn't think there was a single person involved with the fundraiser who didn't know that the majority of the money the two bloggers raised had come from Chloe's network of readers and contacts. She had a lot of power and a long reach. If she decided to start trouble for the foundation, it could be a big problem.

Was her bad relationship with Posy enough to cause her to turn on them?

He hoped not.

He wasn't going to be intimidated into gossiping

about Posy and he wasn't going to stop spending time with her. But it made him antsy to have Chloe watching from the wings.

ALMOST IMMEDIATELY after hitting the last ball, Posy realized she'd let her competitive spirit take over. She wished she could do it over again. She didn't need to get out there and make a spectacle of herself, not in Kirkland, anyway. She could have watched Trey and Shawn and whoever that teenage girl was battle it out.

She saw Chloe and Felicity talking to Wes and she could guess what they were saying.

The kids swarmed her, shouting about their favorite hits and asking her if she wanted to go again. Shawn gave her a high five and Trey handed her a Wiffle ball.

"Game ball," he said with a grin. "You should make Wes sign it for you."

"I'll put it in my trophy case as soon as I get home," she said.

Eventually the group started back toward the basketball court. Deacon was going to make a short speech and there was some kind of cheer they wanted to do before the day ended. She turned the ball over in her hand, thinking about Wes and the look he'd given her right before he threw the last pitch.

The crowd lined up around the basketball courts. Deacon gave a speech about his hopes for the Hand-to-Hand partnerships and his belief that everyone has something to offer. He thanked Wes for all his efforts putting Equipment Day together and Wes waved. Then

Trey and Shawn brought up four mesh bags full of pink basketballs and the kids from the Milton center lined up.

"Ten years ago," Deacon said, "Julia, Wes and I were coaching a basketball team. The girls were having trouble coming together and our record wasn't that great. I take my basketball seriously and I thought if the kids worked harder and with more purpose, we'd start to win. My brother thought we needed a dance."

"All the movie teams have dances," Wes added.

"I set a goal for the girls and told them if they met it, they could have their dance. We'll never know if it was the goal or the dance that made the difference—"

"It was the dance," Wes called.

"But the team got together and ever since then we've taught the dance to kids who come to the Fallon centers. Right now, we want to invite our friends from Kirkland to join us."

They passed out the balls and then the music came on. The dance was more like a basketball-handling display, like something the Harlem Globetrotters would do. Watching the Fallons, Trey and Shawn, and all the kids out there moving to the music, she knew it didn't matter what she called it. What mattered was coming together as a community. All day she'd watched Wes listen to people and see what they needed and then try to make it happen for them. He might be new at his job, but he was a natural. It was clear to her that Kirkland was going to get its Hand-to-Hand center and Wes would be right there to run it.

She wondered what it would feel like to get on the

court with them, with a ball of her own, moving in unison with the rest of their team.

When the song ended, Deacon, Julia and Wes went back to the microphones. "We wanted to take this opportunity," Deacon said, "on a day when the Fallon Foundation came together with Kirkland, to announce an incredibly generous donation."

Wes gestured toward her. "Posy Jones, representing her mother, Trish." Then he found Chloe in the yard and called her name.

She stood next to Chloe and listened to the speech Deacon gave about the small donors and the network of blog readers coming together that was such a great metaphor for the idea behind the Hand-to-Hand centers.

"Thanks to Trish Jones and Chloe Chastain and the community they brought together to raise more than sixty-eight thousand dollars."

She stayed until the clapping ended and then she excused herself while Chloe was talking to Wes and Deacon.

Not many people were leaving, so she had trouble finding her way through the crowd around the courts. Wes came up next to her and before she realized what he was doing, he'd angled her off to one side.

"You're leaving?"

"I have to get home," she said.

"You didn't tell me you're a professional Wiffle ball player. If I knew, I would have given you my really fast stuff instead of those easy ones."

"Smoke, huh?"

"It's a name that strikes fear in my opponents."

"I was terrified. Shawn was shaking. Seriously."

"Hey, at least it was entertaining."

"You know what, Wes? It was," she said. "I had low expectations for this day. I spent my life with a professional do-gooder, so I've been to a lot of events like this, but I've never had such a good time."

"Thanks," he said. "I really wanted it to work out. This was important to my brother."

"What about to you?" she asked.

"Me?" He looked surprised. "I'm happy if he's happy, I guess."

"That's a little lame," she said. Then she added, "Sorry. I didn't mean that. I just— I guess I just wonder what makes Wes Fallon happy besides making sure his brother is happy."

"Go out with me tonight," he said. He looked as if he'd even surprised himself.

"Out?"

"Dinner. Tonight. Are you busy?"

There'd been that one pitch he threw. He stared at her and she stared at him and she hadn't been able to breathe. *Dinner*... He was asking her on a date. She wanted to go. Wanted to kiss him again....

"Dinner? Tonight?"

"Deacon and Julia aren't going back until tomorrow, so we're all going out."

Oh.

Right.

Dinner with his brother. Of course.

"I don't know, Wes. I have a lot to straighten out at my mom's house. You probably want to catch up with Deacon. If I come you'll feel like you have to entertain me."

"I'll tell Deacon no shoptalk. This is just for fun. Come on, Posy." Wes tilted his head and leaned toward her. "I want you to come."

She knew that head-tilting thing was a habit he'd developed because he spent his life talking to people who were shorter than him. But it got to her every time. She couldn't help it. It was just so inviting.

She shouldn't say yes to a dinner just because a cute guy who kissed like the devil tilted his head at her. But she did it anyway.

After the last of the cleanup was finished, Julia drove back to the hotel. Deacon asked Wes if he had some time to talk. The two of them went out to the courts behind the community center. Deacon dribbled the ball out to center court.

Wes made a half-assed attempt to guard his brother when Deacon went up for a shot.

"You know what I never questioned when I was a kid?" he asked.

Deacon shrugged and shot again. "Nope."

"What would happen if you didn't make the NBA. I never doubted you'd make it. Even afterward, I didn't really process exactly how much of a long shot it was. Your draft day just seemed inevitable."

"Because I was a stud."

"Don't forget I also believed in the Easter Bunny during this same blind-faith era."

Deacon spun and dribbled past him, but Wes got in front and blocked his shot. There'd been a time when they'd been almost exactly evenly matched, but in the past two or three years, Deacon lost a step while Wes was still playing professionally. They'd never discussed it. Deacon was the one guy in the world he had no interest in beating on the court.

"So what's your point?"

"Nothing." Wes bounced the ball a few times and then shot. The ball whispered through the net, easy as pie. "But what if you didn't make the NBA? You might have been working in a gas station or flipping burgers or something. Maybe they wouldn't have let you be my guardian. I might have been stuck in foster care till I aged out."

It was bad enough that he'd spent six years in the system and couldn't remember most of it. What if he'd stayed there until he was eighteen? What if all the memories he had of growing up with Deacon—visiting his team locker room, living in his big house with the indoor court, knowing he was safe and wanted—had been replaced by more moves, more rejection? More confirmation that the person he was wasn't acceptable.

"I was going to steal Coach Simon's car and take you away," Deacon said. He clapped his hands and Wes tossed him the ball. "I had a whole plan about crossing the border, moving to Canada, using fake names.

I might have had to grow your hair long and pretend you were a girl."

Wes stopped dead. "Seriously?"

"I always thought you'd look cute in ponytails."

"Screw you. You really thought about running away?"

"Not about the girl thing, but the rest of it? Yeah," Deacon said. "I was too old for the Easter Bunny, Wes. I knew how many ways the NBA thing could go wrong and you couldn't take much more. I wasn't about to leave you in foster care."

Wes smacked the ball out of his brother's hands and shot. The ball bounced off the rim.

"Canada?"

"Don't say I never gave your future any thought."

The ball was all the way across the grass near his office window, so he jogged over to pick it up then he heaved a big pass in to Deacon who caught it on the fly and took it in for a dunk.

"The Fallon brothers," Wes said. "Invincible as always."

"That's actually what I wanted to talk about," Deacon said. "Julia and I are switching things up at home pretty soon. We've done an emergency intervention for this boy named Marcus—he's fifteen and he's a challenging kid, but his home life is a mess. By this time next month, his mom's rights are going to be terminated and he's going to need a permanent foster home. Julia and I really think we can make a difference for him, so we're going to take him in."

Wes smiled. "That's great. The kid is lucky to have a place to land."

"We hope so. But Marcus also has several half siblings. The oldest one is seven and then there are two preschoolers. Julia and I are going to have the whole family, which means we're committing to being full-time for these kids for as long as they need us."

"But you never take young kids."

Deacon nodded. "We prefer the older ones. We've been so busy with the foundation, we needed the flexibility."

"So now these little kids…"

"We can't say no. Sometimes… I don't know, Wes. It's just right for now."

Wes hugged his brother. "That's unbelievable. Way to go, D."

"Well, this is an opportunity for you, too. I'm not going to be able to work the Hand-to-Hand program the way I expected to. We're going to need someone here to set it up, do all the hiring and basically manage the daily operation. There's nobody we'd rather have doing that than you. Hire your buddy Ryan and the two of you can kick this thing into shape."

A cold sweat broke out all over his body. With every word his brother said, Wes felt himself shutting down. Deacon needed him….

He couldn't say no, but did he want to stay here in Kirkland?

Did he have a choice?

HER PHONE RANG when she was getting dressed to meet the Fallons.

"Hey, Posy." It was Wes. "So, bad news. Or maybe not. I guess it depends."

"Depends on what?"

"On if you like karaoke."

In the corner of the room, Angel, who'd appeared early that morning and hadn't escaped yet, shook her stuffed teddy bear until it flew onto the bed.

She felt like the teddy bear in Wes's grip, limp and helpless. The dog stood on her hind legs, paws scrabbling at the mattress. Posy scooped the bear up and threw it down the hall. Angel scrambled after it.

"I'm sensing there's been a change of plans."

"Deacon bet that Julia couldn't list his stats in the quarterfinal game from his last year in the NBA. Turns out she could."

"Impressive."

"Yeah. I should warn you now. Don't bet against Julia." He laughed. "Anyway, she won the right to choose the restaurant tonight and she picked someplace called Finnegan's because it's karaoke night." Wes didn't sound as disgusted as she'd have expected him to be. "You still in?" She was about to say yes, when he added, "Because we can go somewhere else if you're not going to have a good time."

He'd promised her a night on the town after Equipment Day and he'd give it to her even if it meant missing out on his time with his brother. Wes kept his promises.

"I'm a fan of karaoke," she said. "No worries."

Make that one worry. She wasn't wearing the pants she'd planned on for dinner to karaoke night at Finnegan's. Not with Wes.

She opted for a slim skirt that hit just above the knee. On top she layered a spaghetti-strap tank and a deep fuchsia shirt. She added a wide black belt with a funky black-and-white clasp. For shoes, she had two choices— low black heels and lower black heels. She wished she'd packed a pair of real heels, but when she'd planned this trip to Kirkland to visit her mom, she hadn't expected to be moving in and she really hadn't expected to meet someone like Wes.

She looked in the full-length mirror, Angel next to her foot. Her hair looked good—she'd used her curling iron to make big soft waves. Her makeup looked good— her eyes and lips always looked better with a little color defining them. Her chest wasn't as big as she'd have liked, but her stomach was flat and the slim skirt emphasized the curve of her hips and butt. Her legs were good—she'd always liked her legs. Her shoes…well… They were shoes and that was that.

She couldn't fault any of her individual parts. It was just the whole, the complete package, the entire sum of everything that was her. *Big, broad, imposing, strong, tall and all of its synonyms including high, giant and large.* It wasn't that she wanted to be petite. Posy never wished to be her mom's size. It was just that her size combined with her competitive personality were too much. If she were just a little smaller, maybe she would feel more comfortable being herself.

They were going to pick her up and she wanted to be downstairs when they got there. She took one last look in the mirror and then grabbed a black chunky knit sweater. When she put it on, it hid most of her bright shirt and the funky belt. It toned everything down enough that she felt more acceptable.

Angel barked at her when she buttoned the sweater up, but she told the dog to shut up. Angel was small, white and fluffy. She had no clue how it felt to be Posy Jones.

She went downstairs to wait for Wes. She'd made good progress on the kitchen earlier that day and she shoved the finished boxes out of the way so she could lock the sliding glass door. When she tried to turn the lock, it wouldn't catch because a corner of the throw rug was caught in the track. She pushed the door back, but the rug slid along the track with it. When she bent over to tug the fabric loose, Angel shot around her ankle and out into the night.

"Don't do anything I wouldn't do," Posy muttered before she closed the door and locked it.

WHEN THEY GOT to the bar there was a line out the door, so Deacon and Julia dropped them off in front while they went to park the car. She and Wes reached the hostess station just as the other two walked into the bar.

As Deacon and Julia came up behind them, Posy felt the other people in the lobby assessing their group. The Fallons were hard to miss and Julia, in a short, red, sleeveless shift, drew admiring looks.

The hostess behind the podium was in her early twenties. She had a mass of blond hair pulled back and secured in a knot with a pencil. She licked her lips when the four of them came up and Posy watched her do the math, dismiss Deacon as obviously taken, before deciding she had a shot with Wes. Posy recognized the look in the hostess's eye. She'd looked at attractive guys herself just that way. Heck, she'd given Wes that same look. She knew exactly what it meant when the woman leaned over the reservation desk, ostensibly because it was difficult to hear him, but actually because it made the top of her blouse gape, offering a view of a black bra with glittery gold hearts.

Oops.

Oops, my ass.

She wondered if the other woman knew that hussy and hostess shared an awful lot of letters. Posy tugged the sleeves of her sweater down over her wrists.

Wes half turned to her, putting his arm around her back so his fingers rested warm against her waist. He bent his head and his breath was on her ear when he said, "She wants to know if we're planning to sing."

The hostess registered his arm around Posy and her eyes swept Posy from head to toe, taking in the too-big sweater, the too-low heels, the too-much woman.

"It's up to Julia. She wants to sing, right?"

When Wes turned back, the hostess licked her shiny lips again and leaned harder on the podium. One more inch and she might as well just invite him right up inside her shirt.

Posy had been assessed and dismissed.

Wes's hand slid around to the small of her back as the hostess led them through the dining room to a table about three rows back from the stage. She wasn't a person men felt protective of. The funny thing was, she'd always thought it would irritate her to be guided this way. Being steered. But it didn't feel that way at all. It felt like a connection. A very private one.

He put a hand on the back of an empty chair and waited while she smoothed her skirt down and sat. When he sat next to her, he left his hand on the back of her chair so his arm was stretched across her shoulders.

He was dressed in a beautifully cut leather jacket over a slim dress shirt that showed off his chest and trim waist. His dark jeans emphasized the length of his legs. She leaned back, savoring his arm on her, and smiled at the hostess.

The woman snapped the menus on their table and said someone would be with them shortly.

"What a surprise to meet you all here. Hi, Posy." Chloe's sister, Felicity, was stopped next to their table, her eyes on Wes and Deacon even as she held her hand out to Posy. "It's been years, but you still look just the same."

She looked past Felicity's shoulder and saw Chloe coming up to greet them.

Posy introduced Felicity to the others and then Chloe shook hands all around, but when she smiled at Wes, he practically glared at her. Chloe noticed, but she didn't say anything. She left after a few more seconds.

Deacon picked up his menu. "What was that about?" he asked Wes.

"What?"

"The death stare," Julia said. "That woman raised an awful lot of money for us last week."

"Posy's mom started the fundraiser. Without her, we wouldn't have collected a penny," he said. "And it was nothing. I had a conversation with her today and she rubbed me the wrong way, that's all."

Julia picked up her own menu, but she looked from Wes to Posy, a thoughtful expression in her eyes.

THEY DECIDED on a selection of appetizers and one of the wood-fire pizzas that Finnegan's was famous for. Then Julia suggested they get a second pizza and Posy was sure there'd be way too much food, but it turned out Julia knew her brother-in-law very well. Wes ate most of the second pizza himself.

"It's good," was all he said when Deacon made fun of him for having fourths.

Throughout dinner they watched as people got up to do karaoke. The performers included a few high school kids, a bachelorette party that was ordering drinks by the dozen and one or two other couples. Then just as the dishes were being cleared, the emcee announced that they were taking sign-ups for the main event of the evening, the Famous Finnegan's Friday-Night Face-off.

Julia jumped up from the table. "I'm in. Posy? Wes? Are you singing?"

Deacon put his hand over his eyes. "I knew I was

doomed as soon as Julia heard about this." He looked at Posy. "Some lady mentioned it while Julia was helping her kid try on shoes. My wife is a bit of a closeted diva."

"Just for that, I'm signing up for a duet with my husband."

While Deacon begged her to reconsider, Wes leaned in and asked, "What about you, Posy?"

Posy felt the competitive thrill inside. She'd let herself get carried away today playing Wiffle ball. She wouldn't do it again. She was having a good time. She would sit back and watch the singing like a normal person.

Chloe passed their table on her way to sign up. "Posy, you're not signing up? They give out a trophy, you know."

Wes whipped his head around to watch her walk away and then turned back to Posy. "Are you going to just take that?"

She recognized the look in his eye because it was exactly how she felt inside. She wanted to get up and sing and win and then shove the trophy in Chloe's face. Which was exactly how Chloe knew she'd react and was exactly why she needed to shake her head and say, "I don't really feel like singing."

CHAPTER ELEVEN

POSY WAS PROUD OF her self-control. She'd ignored Chloe's taunt and stuck to her guns. She'd watch the contest and that would be that. She picked up her beer and took a sip.

"Do you suck?"

She choked on the mouthful of beer. "What?"

"At singing. Do you suck? Because then I get it. Chloe looked pretty confident and you don't want to look like an idiot. So maybe singing's not your thing."

"No," Posy said. "I don't suck."

"Then let's do this."

He looked so excited, with his eyes lit up and a grin on his lips. She nodded despite what she really thought about it. He told Julia to sign them up to sing together and that was when the regrets settled in. It was fine for him to get up there and care too much and compete. He was an athlete. He'd played professional basketball. People expected guys like him to be serious. He didn't know what it felt like to be a girl who grew too tall and wanted everything too much. She'd never fit in here. Chloe was just waiting to see her make a fool of herself again.

She excused herself and went to the ladies' room.

When she was washing her hands, Julia came in. The other woman leaned against the wall and then pulled away with a face.

"Ugh. That was sticky," she said. "I hope I didn't just catch a disease." She flipped the hot-water tap on and scrubbed her hands. "We're all signed up."

"Good," Posy said.

"Your friend stopped by the table again. She said she won last week."

"She's not exactly my friend."

"I figured that out," Julia said. "I'm actually glad you know it, too. I was worried. You know, Wes is never like that…. Well…almost never."

"Like what?"

"You saw him. When she introduced herself and he was rude to her." Julia rinsed her hands and then pulled a paper towel from the dispenser. "Wes is, well, he's kind of like a sheepdog. Which I mean in the very nicest sense. He's loyal and friendly and pretty much gives anyone a chance. He likes the pack and being part of it. But if he thinks you're screwing with someone he cares about…he changes completely. I still remember the first time I saw him do it. I thought he was just this big, dumb, funny kid and then somebody tried to mess with Deacon and Wes got incensed. His face looked *exactly* like it did when he was dissing Chloe."

She wasn't sure what Julia was implying. "Do you think Chloe said something about Deacon? He mentioned he overheard her today."

Julia tossed her paper towel in the garbage. "Maybe.

But if you want my real guess, I think she said something about you."

Posy's cheeks got warm. Julia studied her quietly, and then said, "He's a very good guy, Posy. But he's never dated anyone who could give him a run for his money. They'd have cheered for him today, but not gotten up there to swing the bat."

Posy nodded, feeling stupid, but completely unable to answer Julia. What could she say?

When Julia left, Posy turned the cold water on and wet her fingers. She patted her cheeks and her forehead. Julia didn't need to tell her that Wes was a good guy. She knew it. That was the problem. He was such a good guy, he was going to stay here in Kirkland, run his brother's charity like a rock star and have the life he deserved. Posy didn't fit here and she never had. It wasn't fair for her to get in between Wes and the life he obviously wanted.

"JULIA FOLLOWED POSY into the bathroom," Deacon said. "Are you nervous?"

Wes flagged down a waitress and ordered another pitcher of beer. Far from feeling nervous, he was having the best day he'd had in a long time.

"You want another soda?" he asked Deacon, but his brother shook his head. Deacon didn't drink. He'd been ten when their dad died and had lived through years of watching him destroy their family because of his addictions. Deacon said he didn't want to take a chance. Wes had been a baby when their father died, so he didn't have the same worries about it that his brother did.

"Did you see her today?" he asked Deacon. "Shawn almost dropped dead when her ball beat his."

"It was pretty sweet. Were you worried?" Deacon asked. "Before she gave you the check?"

"No." He'd been so relieved when she'd handed it over the night before. It was probably part of the reason why his day had gone so well. "Maybe a little. But not about her, just her mom. Did you see the way Chloe baited her? Posy's not going to take that lying down."

Deacon rolled his eyes. "I swear, you and Julia are going to kill me. There's an excellent steak house in Kirkland. Right on the lake. We could be there right now instead of inside this jumped-up pizza place listening to that."

That was the bachelorette party. They'd been drinking from shot glasses for about an hour longer than necessary, judging by the fact that not many of them could read the lyrics from the prompter, let alone sing along to "Landslide." Stevie Nicks would kick all their asses if she heard what they were doing to the song.

Julia planted a noisy kiss on the top of Deacon's head, then slid into her seat next to him, leaning forward for a real kiss. Wes shook his head. They'd never gotten to the stage of their relationship where they weren't completely into each other. Maybe another ten years.

Maybe never.

If they were lucky.

He wanted what Deacon had with Julia. The two of

them worked together, loved each other and shared an agenda that satisfied them both individually and together. Julia quit her job as a guidance counselor about two years after they got married, but she'd been unhappy with the paperwork and regulations that had been slowly taking over her workday. She went to work for Deacon, setting up the tutoring and family-support branches of the Fallon center in Milton and then packaging the plans as modules that could be introduced in the newer Fallon centers. She still did one-on-one tutoring, as well.

She said working at the Fallon centers was her dream job. She complained about the boss every once in a while, but since Deacon was an enthusiastic supporter of every one of her ideas, it was clear she was joking.

She was the one who'd suggested they take in their first foster child. Deacon had hesitated, because he and Wes had seen how complicated foster care could be for kids and the foster families. He wanted to be sure they'd make a positive difference. Julia finally convinced him there wouldn't be guarantees, except the one that any kid they took in was guaranteed to get a fair shot with them.

Wes was pretty sure they were the happiest people he knew. Except on karaoke night. He and Julia sometimes went by themselves, but when Deacon was dragged along, he suffered.

Wes loved it.

"What's the strategy?" he asked Julia.

She pushed Deacon away and said, "It's a single-elimination thing—audience response is the measure."

"Audience response is good. You can never tell if the judges at these things will be impartial."

"You did not just analyze the impartiality of the judging in karaoke contests," Deacon muttered. "Someone shoot me."

Posy came back and stood uncertainly near her chair. He pushed it out to encourage her to sit down. She looked great. Her skirt hugged her curves and even though it wasn't as short as the shorts she'd worn that afternoon, her legs were fantastic.

He always had fun doing karaoke with Julia, but tonight, knowing he was going to sing with Posy, he wanted to crush it.

"There's only one round, so we can't play this safe. First song, best shot. Go for the jugular, right?"

Posy looked from him to Julia. "What are you talking about?"

"How we're going to win," Julia said. "Or at least make sure we beat that Chloe person."

Posy liked the way Julia called her that. She thought she might call her that from now on, herself. She was definitely using it when she talked to her mom next time. If Trish ever decided to give up the silent-retreat farce, that was.

"I'm doing 'Holiday,'" Julia said. Wes gave her a high five. His sister-in-law was an excellent mimic. She had stage presence, too. He'd seen her channel Madonna before and it was uncanny.

"Are we doing a duet?" Wes asked.

"Um, okay," Posy said. "I didn't know you'd be so into this."

"I lived in the basketball dorm in college. We had a curfew on game nights and any night when we were traveling the next day. You can only play so much poker."

"So you sang karaoke?"

"'Rock Band' on Wii. Same principle, except there's a live audience when you do it in a bar."

"Wes is all about the audience," Deacon said. "Maybe I can get a taxi. I feel like I'm getting a headache."

Julia put her hands on either side of his face and kissed him. "Next time don't bet against me, sweetie. You'd think after ten years together—two years married—you'd know this."

"You'd think."

The first act got up. It was a trio of girls who looked as if they might have been in high school or maybe college. They clearly had not taken the audience-response factor into account because they sang a Justin Bieber song and half the guys in the audience booed them on principle. Posy clapped enthusiastically and he raised an eyebrow at her.

"I like his music. I can't help it."

"We're not singing Bieber," he said.

Deacon snapped his fingers. "You know what, that's an excellent idea. Posy, I want you to make Wes sing Bieber." He patted the pocket of the leather jacket he'd draped over the back of his chair. "How's the light in here for videos?"

"No Bieber," Posy agreed.

The second singer, an older guy with a cowboy hat, sang "My Way" and, while he wasn't awful, he was no Frank Sinatra. The audience didn't seem to care for his rendition of the song.

"That's why you should never sing Frank," Julia said. "Everyone who isn't bored by him is a rabid fan."

They sat through two more singers who had some success and then it was Julia's turn. "Wish me luck," she said.

"I hope you win the karaoke contest," Deacon said in an insincere singsong tone.

Wes kicked him under the table.

He watched Posy watch Julia and saw the second that she realized how good his sister-in-law was. "Amazing, right?"

"She doesn't look anything like Madonna, but then she gets up there and just…"

"I know."

When Julia finished, the entire place clapped for her and Deacon was on his feet whistling.

Julia was on top of the leader board when Chloe went up. He had her pegged for a ballad and she didn't disappoint when she launched into a Celine Dion song that always made him cringe.

She carried it off, though, and the applause rating put her even with Julia. There were only two more acts before he and Posy had their chance, so it looked very possible that either Julia or Chloe would be the winner.

Posy touched his arm. "I think we need to go with

something totally over-the-top and fun. We need them ready to yell when we're finished."

"Springsteen?"

"I can't sing Bruce," Posy said. "Can you?"

"I wish."

"Okay, then I nominate 'Friends in Low Places.'"

Wes pumped his fist. "Genius."

When their names were called, he walked behind Posy through the crowd toward the stage. They passed Chloe and her table of women. Several of them called out greetings to Posy. Chloe said, "Cute shoes."

Wes didn't know why that was an insult because he thought Posy's shoes looked perfectly fine, but it definitely was a dig. Posy stopped dead and if he hadn't been watching her hips so closely as they wove through the tables, he might have run right into her.

"What did you say?" she asked Chloe.

"Cute. Shoes."

Two of the women leaned out to get a better look at Posy's feet and Wes glanced down again, but he still couldn't see anything wrong.

Posy tossed her hair over her shoulder and continued toward the stage. When they got there, Wes told the emcee what song they wanted and then turned to see that Posy was unbuttoning the big sweater she'd been wearing. Underneath she had on a bright pink shirt. The top three or four buttons were undone and he had a clear view of the tight black tank top layered below and the gentle swell of her breasts underneath. She was put together so perfectly.

"Ready?" she asked.

Was he ever.

They kicked ass.

Posy owned the stage the same way she owned the plate that afternoon. He actually stumbled over the lyrics at the top of the second chorus when Posy pointed her mic into the crowd and got them singing along. She was shimmying to the music, and watching her hips pump from side to side completely distracted him. Luckily he recovered and the crowd didn't seem to care. They were as into her as he was.

When they were finished, the applause meter put them ahead of Julia in first place. The emcee brought their trophy out and Wes stepped back so Posy could grab it. She didn't waggle it in Chloe's direction, which he would have done. She was obviously more mature than he was.

When the emcee asked what they wanted to do for an encore, he didn't even ask Posy, he just said the first song that came to mind. It had been on his mind since he and Posy first started discussing what to sing.

"We'll sing 'Faithfully' by Journey."

Posy ALMOST DROPPED the trophy. Singing with Wes had been amazing. He had a great voice and he knew how to work the crowd. She'd gotten to stand with him and see Chloe's face when the emcee declared them the winners. That had been enough, she thought. She didn't need any more.

Then the first notes of "Faithfully" started and Wes

held the mic near his mouth, singing right to her and she didn't know what to do. She missed her first cue. Wes sang his line and then took her hand and somehow she found her voice.

She'd never sung a duet like this with anyone in public. Never in private, either. She'd always been on her own. Tonight, though, Wes had been with her when she showed Chloe up and now he was with her again, singing to her, his thumb rubbing across the inside of her wrist while he sang.

Posy forgot about the crowd. Forgot about Chloe and the other Kirkland women at her table. Forgot about her sensible heels, the ones designed to help her fit in, and she sang.

When they were finished, the applause was louder than it had been for their winning song.

Wes pulled her close and kissed her. His lips touched hers gently and then a bit harder. His hands settled on her waist and when he broke the kiss, he pressed his fingertips into her hips for a brief second before he faced the crowd and bowed again.

He held her hand as they left the stage. They could have avoided Chloe's table, but he pulled her right past so the other woman had to acknowledge them.

"Congratulations, Posy," she said. "Just like old times, isn't it?"

He kept holding her hand as they left the restaurant.

Deacon and Julia went to get the car and Wes said, "Come here." He pulled her by the hand and the two of them went around the corner of the building into a narrow alley between Finnegan's and the bank next to it. He leaned against the brick wall of Finnegan's and bent his head to kiss her. Before she could think, his hands were in her hair and stroking down her back, squeezing her hips and sliding down the front of her thighs. She kissed him back, straining toward him, releasing all the emotion she'd felt during the song. Wanting to feel him, wanting him to feel her.

He moaned and tugged, pulling her closer to him. He was hard and his erection pressed against her with tantalizing urgency. She wanted to touch him. Wanted more of him, all of him that she could get.

"Okay," he said against her lips. "Okay. One minute."

He straightened, breaking their kiss, and looked out toward the street. "My brother's going to be here any second." She didn't move. She didn't want this moment to end. He kissed her again, dipping his head and pressing his lips against hers with the same need she felt.

"Deacon," she managed to say. "The car."

They made it out of the alley with a few seconds to spare.

Julia gave them a questioning look when they got in the backseat, but didn't say anything.

His brother and sister-in-law were staying in a hotel downtown, so he said he'd drive Posy home if they dropped them both off at his place.

She wasn't paying much attention to the driving arrangements until Deacon and Julia honked their horn and drove away.

"Why didn't you just let them drive me home? It's not that much more driving."

"Because I didn't know how else I could invite you up to my place."

Oh.

Because of that. Why didn't he say so?

"I haven't had that much fun in a really long time, Posy. I'm not ready for it to end." He squeezed her hand. "Are you?"

She followed him up the stairs to the apartment over Mrs. Meacham's garage. The light was on outside the kitchen door and she stood on the step below the landing while he dug the keys out of his pocket. His leather jacket stretched tight across his shoulders. His hands made quick work of the lock and with one firm twist the door was open.

She'd seen those same hands earlier today, gently tying shoes on small feet. She'd seen them juggling Wiffle balls and pouring beer. She'd felt them on her hips and back and thighs.

He had no idea what he was getting into with her. She knew he hadn't understood what made her so mad about Chloe's crack about her shoes. But she'd been hurt. She'd spent so much of her life in Kirkland covering up and trying to fit in and trying to compress herself into the space she was allowed to have. It hadn't always worked. With Chloe and girls like her, she'd been mocked on both ends, when she let herself go and when she tried to be more in the norm.

Like with her shoes tonight.

Wes's apartment was not what she'd expected. Her Google search before she met him turned up images of him with models and professional athletes. He'd lived in Europe. Grown up with a brother who was an NBA star. She'd expected his place to be luxurious, or at least nicer than her own apartment, but when he said he lived over Mrs. Meacham's garage, he meant exactly that.

The door opened onto a small galley kitchen. Open shelves held a set of white plates and glass tumblers. The stove had two burners and a small fridge was tucked next to the sink. Only the expensive coffeemaker on the counter hinted that someone other than a grad student lived here. The space was cramped, obviously not designed for two tall people who were intent on sharing the same square inch of floor.

He reached around her, the cool leather of his jacket skimming her arm, and flicked a switch, turning a soft light on over the counter. With one arm around her waist, he tossed his keys toward a tray on the windowsill. The throw tipped him forward and her chest met his as he tightened his arm around her waist.

Her arms went around him. She grabbed a fistful of the jacket at the small of his back and ran her other hand from his shoulder to his waist. The combination of smooth leather over hard muscle was so sensual she instinctively pressed closer to him. He bent his head, his hands on her shoulders, and kissed her. He started at her hairline, his lips skimming across her hair and forehead, sending a shiver through her. She didn't feel small next to him, but she had so rarely been with a guy who was tall enough to kiss the top of her head, and the shift in her usual perspective was exciting.

He continued kissing down the side of her face and when he nuzzled under her ear, she tipped her head back and he licked and kissed down her sensitive throat. He was turning her on so much. She forced herself to keep her hands still because if she let loose with everything she was feeling, she might scare him off.

"Wes," she murmured. "You don't—"

"Don't what?" She'd been about to tell him he didn't have to do this but she changed her mind. She wanted this night with him.

"Nothing."

He moved back and kissed her on the mouth, his lips firm and warm, giving her infinite pleasure as she kissed him back. Kissing was safe. She could respond to his mouth with hers. But she had to keep tight control over the impulse she had to grab him harder, to wrap one of her legs around his.

He walked them backward out of the kitchen, through a dark space she assumed was the living room, and then through an open doorway into his bedroom. He kept kissing and stroking her the entire way. It was killing her to keep her hands still. To remember to touch him gently. To be in control. Not want too much.

He paused and reached behind him to flick a switch. The bedside lamps came on, shedding a warm, soft light across his big platform bed.

In three steps, her knees hit the edge of the mattress and they stopped. He'd pulled her hair back away from her face, smoothing it down across her shoulders, stroking his fingers across the back of her neck. Then he pulled away from her lips and looked into her eyes.

"I wanted to touch your hair the first second we met. You're gorgeous. Every. Single. Inch." He punctuated his statement with kisses, on her lips, her neck and finally, behind her ear where he'd lifted the hair away to expose her sensitive spot. "Sorry about the close quarters. I had to get a new bed because the one Mrs. M. had in here was too small."

He sat and tried to pull her into his lap, but she resisted. He was plenty strong enough to hold her, but she never felt comfortable when someone else could feel her whole weight. She wanted him to focus on her one part at a time.

"Do you want to go back in the living room?" he asked. "We don't have to—"

"This is fine. This is…lovely."

He gave her a funny look, turning his head sideways and half grinning as if he wasn't sure if there was a punch line coming, but then he stood again. His lips met hers and he put his arms around her, gathering her in toward him, his fingers pressing into her skirt. He moaned and started trying to tug the jacket down off his shoulders, but he couldn't get a good angle and he moaned again, this time in frustration.

"Let me," she whispered. She put her hands over his to still them and then slid her right hand up inside the jacket, lifting the leather off his shoulder and peeling it down. She went slowly, savoring each glancing touch of her skin on his before letting the jacket fall to the floor.

He worked the buttons of her shirt, opening it down to her belt and then fumbling at the clasp. When he had it open, the belt came off and he pulled her shirt down over her arms, leaving her in just her tank top. She shivered and watched as he unbuttoned his own shirt, opening three buttons before getting impatient and yanking it over his head.

His muscles were well defined and a dusting of dark curls tempted her hands forward to touch him. She ran her hands over his chest and then up over his shoulders. He had a long surgical scar on one shoulder and she touched it gently then slid her hands up his neck and through the soft brush cut of his hair. She'd expected his short hair to be bristly, but it was actually smooth, like a cat's fur. She rubbed her hands through it forward and back.

"Still feels weird to me," he said. "But better with you touching it."

He put his hands on the button at the back of her skirt and then made eye contact. "Is this okay?"

She wished he'd stop asking for permission. She wanted him and he wanted her and she wished that was enough. She didn't want to keep being reminded that she was taking as much as she was giving here. She nodded and he unbuttoned and unzipped. Her skirt hit the floor and she went still, hating this first moment when a guy saw her whole body without the camouflage of clothing.

The first guy she'd ever been with, a drunk boy she'd
met at a college house party, had whistled and said,
"That's a whole lot of woman" when she took her clothes
off for him. He hadn't noticed that she cried all the way
through her first sexual experience.

Sex was irrevocably tied to feeling too big in her body.
As much as she'd worked to get over it in subsequent relationships, the feeling was always there, an imprint on
her psyche that she couldn't erase. She tried to press the
memory back down, to get herself back into this moment with Wes. He was different. She didn't feel that
way about herself.

Wes was too busy with his own belt and jeans to notice that she was ashamed. But when he was stripped
down to just his boxers, he looked up at her and said,
"What's wrong?"

Damn. She was messing this up and she wanted it.
She wanted Wes. She was here with Wes and needed to
keep her mind here with him, too. It was just so hard to
keep her thoughts under control when Wes insisted on
trying to drive her into a frenzy. She couldn't be ratio-
nal and be with Wes at the same time.

"Nothing."

"What happened tonight? Right before we went onstage, Chloe said something to you and you changed.
What did she say?"

Posy sighed. "You want me to explain an insult to
you?"

"If you don't, I might think you're just psycho, because I could have sworn she said, 'Cute shoes.' Most people would take that as a compliment."

Her pride. Her godforsaken pride begged her not to tell him. But she wasn't hiding anymore.

She leaned down and picked up one of her shoes. He touched her back, trailing his fingers on her skin and she almost dropped the shoe.

"Low heels. Sensible shoes. Not cute. They were meant to help me fit in with the other women who are constructed on a completely different scale, and Chloe and I and every other woman in the room knew the shoes were futile because I don't fit in and I never have. I'm too much."

He took the shoe from her and held it. "Wow. All that from a pair of shoes. Chloe's complicated. But you're right. Awful."

She waited for him to say something comforting, something to make her feel better, but he just dropped the shoe on the floor and looked at her.

His eyes ran from her hair to her neck, down over her breasts, and all the way down past her thighs to her bare toes. She felt her face go red.

He touched her shoulder, stroking from her neck across her collarbone and across the breadth of her shoulder.

"The next time we wipe the stage with Chloe at karaoke, I expect you to wear real heels. Why try to fit in with a bunch of ordinary people when you are extraordinary?"

She didn't know what to say. Every time she thought

she knew what to expect, he swerved and then it turned out he was doing the exact right thing. The perfect thing for her.

He toyed with the strap of her tank top, sliding his finger underneath and running it down to dip into the scoop neckline where he could skim the tops of her breasts.

"Are you sure you want to do this?"

"Yes. Please, Wes."

"It's just, before…when we were onstage and then outside the bar, you were so into it. Into us. And now I feel like you're forcing yourself. We don't have to do this, Posy. I can drive you home if you've changed your mind."

"No. It's not that. I want to be with you."

"Show me?" He did that head-tilt thing—drawing her in and making her feel special at the same time. He put his lips against hers and breathed, "Come on, Posy. If we're going to do this, let's do it."

He cupped her bottom and squeezed, pulling her toward him. She tried to kiss him, but he pulled his head back.

"Touch me. Touch me like you can. Like you want to."

She shuddered. The need in his voice, the tight pull of his hands, it was all too much.

"Posy. That day on the basketball court…" He closed his teeth on the skin at her shoulder. He bit her, not hard, but not gently. "I never did anything like that with a woman. I haven't stopped thinking about it. We went somewhere together. Come on, Posy. Forget everything else. Go with me now." He bit her again and she remembered how she'd felt on the basketball court. She hadn't hurt him. Hadn't overwhelmed him. He'd been ready for her—all of her and they'd pushed each other.

She lifted her hands to his shoulders and dragged him toward her. He grinned at her. A full-on, wicked and purposeful grin, which was lost as she covered his lips with hers.

She cupped the front of his boxers and squeezed. This time he shuddered and she lifted her leg to wrap around his hip, the way she'd been wanting to do since she first stepped foot in his tiny kitchen.

His hips rocked forward. She pushed against him. Their hands were roaming, busy squeezing and teasing. Now on him, now on her, moving together and driving each other onward.

She was ready for him and more than ready when they wound up on the bed finally. He'd opened a condom and was lying half on her, half off, supporting himself with one arm and using his fingers to drive her higher to an orgasm. She pulled him down, rocking him off balance so he'd have to cover her, press her down, so she could press back against him. It was rough, but so incredibly sexy. Every time she demanded more from Wes, more heat, more strength, more touch, he had it to give and she knew he wouldn't run out.

She climaxed against his hand and then he slid inside, pumping once into her before pausing.

"Okay."

"Go, Wes. More."

HE ALMOST CAME when she said that. Posy made him crazy. She was the woman he'd fantasized about but had never been able to find. The one who wasn't intimidated by him, who didn't need him because he was bigger and stronger, but needed what he could give her just the same.

Everything about her turned him on and he'd been holding on to his self-control the whole time he stroked her to climax. He wanted this night to be better than good for her and he didn't trust himself to last long once he was inside her.

He rocked against her, holding her breast, kneading and rolling the nipple and watching Posy climb back to the place he'd taken her just minutes ago. This time they were going together. He increased his speed and she responded by wrapping those gorgeous long legs around his waist and holding him hard against her. He felt her thighs squeeze against his bare skin and he lost it, driving into her one last time and then panting through to the finish.

She kept up her own rhythm for another few seconds and then she shuddered against him.

He couldn't speak.

That was what he'd felt the first time she'd touched him on the basketball court. He didn't know what happened earlier, where she went when she shut down the way she did, but when she came back to him, it was the most amazing sex he'd ever had.

He let himself fall forward, burying his face in the soft waves of her hair spread on his pillow.

"Wow. Posy. That was…"

She didn't answer.

He wondered if she was asleep.

Then she said, "My mom stole the fundraiser money."

CHAPTER TWELVE

HIS ROOM WAS DARK and they were tangled in each other. His heart was still racing enough to think maybe he'd misheard her even though he knew in the pit of his stomach that she'd said exactly what he thought she had.

"I need one minute and then we can go again. Don't move."

"Wes? Did you hear me? I'm so sorry. I paid the money back, so I thought I wouldn't have to tell you, but that was wrong. She was wrong."

"Okay. So let's forget you told me for a few more hours and do some more of this."

"Wes."

He pulled back. "That was amazing."

"I know. That's why I have to tell you this before it gets any further. Wes—she took it all and gave it to a friend of hers who basically stole it." She pulled away from him but he still held her.

"She gave away our money." He buried his face in her neck. "The money that Chloe, the barracuda, helped raise?"

"Yes."

He pulled back reluctantly.

"Why?"

"Why did she do it?"

"No. Why didn't you tell me?" He'd sat up on the edge of the bed, his back to her. "Why did you lie to me?"

"She does these things and I clean them up. It's never been this bad before and I just thought if I paid the money back, it would all go away. But that was before I got to know you."

"Why didn't she go to the cops when her friend took the money from her?"

"Because my mom gave it to her free and clear. There was no contract, she just trusted her," Posy said. "The woman declared bankruptcy. Maybe eventually there'd be a way for my mom to make a claim, but it wouldn't help now."

"So when Deacon was looking for the check and Chloe kept saying something fishy was going on, your mom was sitting there with a zero balance in the fund-raising account? If someone found out, the Hand-to-Hand project would be ruined. It could kill our whole foundation."

"You're right." She moved away from him, sliding backward toward the edge of the bed. "Nobody knows, though. And I looked at the records. You have every penny my mom raised, I promise."

"It's not about the money, Posy. That foundation is my brother's dream. Deacon trusted me to take care of this and I trusted you. I told you that."

He rolled off the bed, grabbed his jeans and went into the adjoining bathroom, slamming the door behind him. After he was cleaned up, he put his jeans on and went back out. She'd gotten her skirt and tank top back on. The pink blouse hung open from her shoulders. Sitting at the foot of his bed, her hair in messy waves, her clothes undone, she looked beautiful, but off-limits.

"The money isn't the issue. The foundation is the issue. If the Fallon Foundation loses its reputation because our donations are being embezzled, you know what? Deacon, Julia, me…we'll all be fine. Deacon's rich as hell and I've got more than enough plus a college degree. But if the Fallon centers have to close or cut back, there's a whole bunch of communities with real needs that are going to be screwed. Real-live kids and families and neighborhoods that rely on us to bring them programs that make their lives better."

"I'm sorry, Wes. I wanted to tell you."

"But you didn't. You have the luxury because you grew up here with your mom and your dad and your pretty suburban house. You don't worry every day about how you're going to get through the next one."

"I should have told you the minute I found out, but I kept thinking I could fix it. Things with my mom have always been complicated and I thought…I hoped…that this time, if I could fix this one thing and get her to sell Wonders, she could have a fresh start. I wanted her to have a fresh start."

She put her hands over her face. He was so furious he couldn't make himself shut up.

"You want to talk about fresh starts? Deacon didn't learn to read until he was almost thirty. Did you know

that? When he was a little kid, he was so completely
stressed out he couldn't focus in school. The other kids
were learning to read and he was exhausted from worrying all the time. His entire life has been impacted by
the fact that our family was always on the verge of disaster and he carried too much of the burden practically
from the time he could walk. Maybe there's someone
like him coming into a Fallon center. Maybe the kid gets
a meal. Has someone responsible to look after his baby
brother while he plays some basketball. There's someone there who notices that he can't do his homework and
gets him some help. So there you go. The Fallon center
kid has a life, a *real life,* and you and your mom never
gave a single thought to how her creative bookkeeping
would impact those children." He paused. "You lied to
me. Over and over."

"I was only lying while I got the money to pay you
back."

"We have the money, but this story is out there, Posy.
Your mom knows. Her friend knows. You know. Chloe
suspects something. Everything Deacon worked for is
in jeopardy if someone finds out. Even though you paid
the money back, your mom still stole it. It's still a crime
and he could still have your mom arrested."

She flinched. "Would you really press charges?"

He'd screwed this up. Every time Deacon asked him
if the finances were in good shape he'd reassured him.
He wasn't going to get between his brother and Trish
Jones again. "It's Deacon's call."

He left the bedroom. In the kitchen, he grabbed his

keys because she'd need a ride home, but when she emerged, she said she'd already called a cab. They stood in awkward silence in his too-small kitchen for a few minutes and then she said she would wait downstairs.

"It's the middle of the night. You can't stand around on the street by yourself."

"I can't stand here with you, Wes." Her lower lip trembled. She was trying not to cry. For the first time since she'd laid this bombshell on him, he felt for her. The kitchen was tiny and he was still very obviously angry. He imagined she could feel the anger rolling off him. He was making himself uncomfortable and it would be a hundred times worse for her. He didn't need to punish her when it was really her mom who should have to deal with him.

She waited on the sidewalk behind his apartment while he sat on the top of the steps and watched her. She kept her back turned, but every few seconds she'd lift a hand to her face. He didn't need to hear her to know she was crying. He was already coming down from his anger. He'd learned way back in those foster care years that getting angry was almost always a losing proposition. It didn't do much except cut you off from other people. He much preferred to work things out. Except this thing with Posy hit every one of his buttons. Deacon. Family. His own pride. His... God, he hated that he'd started to care about Posy. That just made everything worse.

When the cab came, she looked as if she almost

turned to him but changed her mind. The cab door closed and she was gone.

How many times had someone closed the door on him in his life? He'd thought he was getting somewhere in Kirkland. Making connections and finding a place.

He never liked the first few minutes after someone left. He wasn't an idiot. He knew that getting moved all those times when he was young, not being allowed to live with Deacon—who was the only person he counted on—had done a number on him. It didn't make it hurt any less when the door closed on another person he'd just started to care about.

He couldn't go to bed. Not in his room where her scent still lingered and every surface held the imprint of her or them together. He didn't know when he'd be able to sleep in there again, but not that night, for sure.

He went down to Mrs. Meacham's yard and sat in the Adirondack chair. The stars were out and he stared up at them for a few minutes, but that was all the sitting still he could take.

He went back to his apartment and grabbed his keys and phone. Then he drove over to the Kirkland Community Center. He'd go over the records of donations Posy gave him. He'd check and recheck every detail until he could get in touch with Deacon before he and Julia drove back to Milton later that morning.

He flipped the lid of his laptop open and slid the binder out from the shelf where he'd filed it. He was such an idiot. Deacon had once again given him a handout, offered him this job while he was working out what he wanted to do now that he wasn't playing anymore. And of course Wes was sitting on the embezzlement of the entire fundraiser and he'd never known a thing.

His phone rang about ten minutes after he sat down. He turned the screen over and saw Posy's number. He almost let it go, but the building was so quiet and dark. He wondered if it was possible he'd made this whole stupid evening up.

"Hello?"

"Sorry to call you so late. I…I thought you might be sleeping."

"I can't."

"I can't, either." She sighed.

Neither of them spoke for a few seconds. He wished this could be a normal conversation. He wished he could go to her house and pick her up and drive off with her and put this disaster behind them.

"Posy?"

"I know I have no right to ask you for any favors, but I just hoped that if Deacon does decide to call the police…could you call me first? We won't do anything stupid, I promise. I'd want to be with her, that's all. If they arrested her."

Wes pressed his hand to his temple and then smoothed it back across his hair. He couldn't stand this. Why had she lied to him? Her mom was the one in the wrong and he and Posy were the ones paying for her actions. He wanted to tell Posy to let her mom take her chances, but he couldn't. Deacon had stood by him through some stupid things when he was younger. Sure, he'd been mad, but he'd never have left Wes on his own. Family was family.

"I'll call you. Promise."

That little hitch he'd heard in his kitchen was back when she said, "Thanks, Wes."

He hung up and said quietly, "No problem."

DEACON DIDN'T GET MAD. Wes brought all the paperwork to the suite he and Julia were staying in at the hotel. He expected his brother to blow up, but instead Deacon said, "How's Posy?"

"Posy? She's... I don't know. She went home a while ago."

Julia paced from the window to the desk and back again. "This is awful. What was her mother thinking?"

"From what Posy said, it sounds as if she wasn't thinking. She thought she could trust this friend and she has a history of getting herself into sticky situations."

"So where did the money come from? Who actually paid it?"

Wes shrugged. "I think Posy raised it somehow. She said she's selling her mom's house and closing the store, but there's quite a bit of debt on both and she hasn't gotten the money from them yet."

"You didn't find out where the money came from?" Julia asked. "That's an awfully big check for someone to write on short notice."

Posy had said almost that exact thing when she gave it to him. Her hands had been shaking. He'd forgotten that.

He'd been so mad, he hadn't even thought about how awful this must have been for Posy. He knew better than to get that angry. He usually had much more control.

"We need to call Vic and our lawyer and be sure we're covered in case the information gets out somehow. If we can provide an accounting of all the donations, we're probably technically okay. We never authorized the fundraiser, so we can get some distance there, too. We just need to be sure that there isn't some hidden liability that I can't see."

Victor Odenthal was Wes's agent, but he was also on the board of directors of the Fallon Foundation and Deacon's business partner in his string of physical-therapy centers. He was almost an honorary Fallon.

Wes put his hands in his pockets. He'd thought about how to say this next piece and had come up with a dozen different options, but in the end he said simply, "I'm sorry I didn't stay on top of this, Deacon. I know I let you down."

Julia stuttered in her pacing but picked the rhythm back up again, careful not to look at either him or Deacon.

"You didn't let me down. Posy's mom is a nut job, but I don't blame you for not seeing this. Before they paid us, I thought there was something screwy going on, but I never suspected she'd cleaned the account entirely out. Who does that?"

"I thought something was off, too. I should have followed up more carefully."

Deacon stood. He put his hand on Wes's shoulder.

"Come on, man. You were following up. You haven't even been here for two weeks yet and we already know the worst, right? It's all cleanup from here. We'll get through it."

"But I—"

"Enough. Nothing here is your fault. We have to get the Hand-to-Hand center set up, and that's where we need to put our focus."

"Okay," Wes said. He still felt like crap, but he didn't need to whine to Deacon about it anymore. He needed to do better. That was all. "What are you going to do about Trish?"

"I'm not sure. That's one of the things we need to talk to Vic about."

"If you're calling the cops, will you let me know? I promised Posy I'd give her a heads-up. She wants to be there with her mother."

Deacon shook his head. "I certainly hope to God we don't have to have anyone arrested. This…" He picked up the stack of donor records. "It's bad, but I'm going to tell Victor to give us the best option, not the biggest punishment."

Julia had been quiet, but now she asked, "Is Posy okay? I imagine she didn't want to come with you this morning, but I don't want her hurt in all this. I really like her."

Wes stared at her. "Julia, she lied to us. She lied right to my face and she—"

"She was trying to protect her mother and she paid every penny back, as far as we know."

"Yes, but—"

"I'm with Julia," Deacon said. "I can understand doing what she did for family."

"I hope if I embezzle from a charity that you will beat the crap out of me, Deacon, not try to cover it up."

"Oh, I'd kill you. But that would be between me and you. I wouldn't want to see you go to jail."

Wes wasn't sure what to say. Deacon was in a different place than he was on this issue. Julia stepped in. "Deacon, would you mind getting us some coffee? I want to talk to Wes alone for a minute."

Deacon pulled a button-down shirt on over his T-shirt and scooped his wallet off the table near the door. "You want something, Wes? You look awful."

Wes shook his head. "I love it when you go all maternal on me like that."

"Don't mock me or I will take back my offer."

"Fine," Wes said. "Thanks."

After Deacon left, Julia pulled the upholstered chair around so she could face him where he was sitting on the edge of the desk.

"You're wearing the same clothes you had on last night."

He glanced down. "I didn't sleep."

"Except your shirt is on inside out."

"What the—" He hadn't noticed. "Yeah. I guess I took it off while I was lying down."

"Is that what the kids are calling it these days?"

"Julia, what are we doing?"

"I'm counseling you. I hardly ever get to do this any-more, so I thank you for helping me stay in practice."

"I don't need counseling."

"Wes, you like Posy and that's okay. She seems like a really, really nice person."

He clenched his hands into fists and had to force himself to relax again. "No, Julia. She lied to me. She lied to me and I believed her and told Deacon every-thing was okay. I can't be with someone like that. How can I ever trust her?"

"Are you sure you're upset that she lied to you or is it because you feel like you let Deacon down? Some-day you're going to meet someone and she's going to be the right woman for you. You're going to have to let her come first—before Deacon."

"I know," he said.

"Before the debt you think you owe Deacon, too."

He shook his head. "I'm not putting some stranger ahead of my family," he said, but even as the words came out of his mouth, he remembered Posy and the way she'd looked waiting for the cab, crying by her-self. He'd wanted to run away with her and leave both of their families behind.

Julia leaned forward and hugged him. "Everyone always says you were wild when you were little. You know, all the running away and the fighting. I know part of it was that you were so scared and upset and missing Deacon."

She patted his back and he felt ridiculous. He was twenty-eight years old, for Pete's sake, and Julia was treating him like he was five. On the other hand, his night sucked, he was exhausted and upset, and Julia really knew how to give a good hug. Plus, she liked to think she was his second mother or maybe his big sister. So he indulged her. He let her hug him because it made her happy.

"Don't you think, though, that part of it was just who you are. You're a little wild, Wes. You're competitive and you like to be in the spotlight and as much as you want to support Deacon, you really like to be in charge. I hope you find someone who loves those things about you."

THE THREE FALLONS WOUND UP going out for brunch and then they had a conference call with Victor. They decided that they would get in touch with Trish and see if she had a lawyer. They wanted to make sure she wasn't in charge of any more fundraisers, sanctioned or not. It wasn't as if there was a way to blackball a do-gooder-gone-wrong without dragging her name through the mud, but they wanted to see if it was possible to work out a deal. In the meantime, Wes would go full steam with the last few pieces of the Hand-to-Hand deal and bring that project home.

They had a plan hammered out by late afternoon when Deacon and Julia drove back to Milton.

He went to his apartment. He still didn't feel like going upstairs, so when he saw Mrs. Meacham in the yard, he went in and sat with her. She seemed happy to see him, but while they were talking, she called him

Wayne. He was pretty sure that was her husband's name. He made sure she got inside okay and then he heated up some chicken and rice he found in a container in the fridge. He even sat with her while she had her dinner, but eventually she was ready to watch her evening shows and he had to head back to his own place. He was going to have to tell Jay that his mom might need to get checked. She was an awesome lady, but it made him nervous to think of her being alone in her house if her mind was starting to wander.

He grabbed a bottle of water out of his fridge and turned the TV on. He couldn't find a game, but there was a replay of an old Celtics and Lakers championship game on ESPN Classic. He sank into the cushions on the couch and crossed his feet on the slightly beat-up coffee table. His sleepless night was finally catching up with him and he figured he could sleep right here on the couch, avoiding his bedroom and all associations with Posy for one more night.

He wondered what she was doing. Her mom was crazy and she didn't seem to have any other family.

He remembered what he'd said when Julia told him that he might be able to forgive Posy if he remembered what *he* would do for his family.

"That's the issue," he said. "You're my family. Not her."

And he meant it. Deacon and Julia were his family and he'd do anything, or give anything, for them. The trouble was, the two of them drove off back to their house in Milton where they had their life together. They were his family, but they were their own family, too. And he was alone.

CHAPTER THIRTEEN

THE CAB HAD DROPPED Posy off at around four-thirty that morning. It had been that odd time of night when dawn was coming so close you could almost see it, but the night was still holding tight to the sky and the dark corners of the yard. The motion light on her mom's garage had come on as she went up the driveway and she'd jumped when a pair of eyes glowed from under the bush near the front porch. Angel had slipped out of the shadows and waited for her to open the door.

"I hope you had fun," Posy had muttered. "But you better not have eaten anyone's lingerie tonight. I can't deal with any more terrible behavior."

She'd gotten in the shower and let the hot water pound down on her neck and back, wishing it would do something to relieve the tension. But all it had done was remind her of how wonderful Wes's hands felt on her.

She was surprised that she actually fell asleep, but she'd woken again before eight, with the early-spring sunlight pouring across her face through the open curtains.

So much of what Wes had said to her the night before had been true. She hadn't been thinking about the foundation or how her mom's crime might impact their projects beyond the lost money. She'd been so focused on clearing up her mom's mess.

One thing in particular was nagging at her, though, and it was a piece of information that had fallen into place with some other things Wes had said about his life and his brother. Before she met them, she'd assumed that the Fallons grew up the way she did, or almost the way she did. Some suburban life somewhere with a home and a stable set of adults. She knew their parents had died and after Deacon got drafted, he'd raised Wes, but now she thought she'd drastically underestimated the struggles they'd had before Deacon's big break.

Wes had been right that she hadn't really thought about the mission of the foundation or what it meant to his family beyond the fact that it was their work. The kids she'd met yesterday were in her mind now. Whatever happened with her mom was out of her hands, but she owed it to Wes to show that she'd heard what he said, that it made a difference in her.

Angel was curled into a ball in the window seat in the bay window at the front of the house, but Posy put kibble in her bowl anyway. Then she called her cousin.

She drove out to the Knoll and met Maddy in the sitting room on the first floor of her dormitory.

"Your mom is still on silent retreat," Maddy said.

"Well, that ends today," Posy said. "The Fallons know what she did."

"Oh, mercy," Maddy whispered. "What are they going to do?"

"I don't know. Wes said he'd call me if they're going

to the police, so I hope I can be here if she does get arrested, but I know what I need to do."

"I'm washing the floor in the big chapel today. Want to help?"

"No." Posy laughed. "But I think penance is exactly the thing for me today."

The sisters at the Knoll believed that hard work was good for the soul, so "washing the floor in the big chapel" meant they were on their hands and knees with brushes and buckets of soapy water scrubbing miles of flagstones. Posy's back was killing her before the first twenty minutes were over, but she kept her head down and scrubbed doggedly. She relished the work, happy thinking that she was scrubbing away some of the wrong she'd done.

"I spent the morning reading everything I could find about the Fallon Foundation and this new project, the Hand-to-Hand thing. Then I called Wyatt and talked to him about getting the Hotel Marie involved. They do corporate giving and I thought of a way I can spin this Hand-to-Hand idea to work with the Hotel Marie's corporate image."

"Can Wyatt do anything about getting money, though?"

"Not him, but he thought it was a fantastic idea and he's going to take it to the folks who make these decisions. He's really excited about it. He told me his mom was a maid in a motel when he was a kid and he spent a lot of time hanging around the rooms while she cleaned. He's heard about the Fallon centers, which sound like the kind of place he wished he could have gone when he was growing up."

Posy swiped her brush across the last stone in her current row and slid her bucket back. "The Hotel Marie slogan is 'Just like coming home.' So, what if they gave a donation for every stay during a certain period of time? The donations could be tagged 'From our home to yours.' Because the Hand-to-Hand centers are all about communities helping communities. Wyatt said he thinks they'll be able to do something."

"I think it sounds great, Posy. Really great." Maddy dipped her brush into the bucket and scattered water on the next row of flagstones. "So that's one issue you've solved in an afternoon. What are you going to do about your mom?"

Posy almost negated all the penance she'd done with her scrubbing by saying a bad word right in the church. She bit her lip, though, and shook her head. She was going to have to confront her mother today and she couldn't imagine that it would go anything but badly.

SHE KNOCKED and her mom opened the door, a smile on her face. "Hello—" she said, but when she saw Posy, she clamped her lips together and pointed at her throat and her mouth and shook her head no to indicate that she couldn't speak.

"Can it, Mom. I know you've been talking the whole time you've been here. Besides, we're in trouble."

Trish put her hands to her cheeks and widened her eyes, like the heroine in a silent movie who sees the train barreling down the tracks toward her. She shook her head again.

"Fine. If you don't want to talk, I'll talk and you can...play charades or whatever it is you're doing."

Trish pointed to the sign on the wall of her room that said, Silent Retreat in Progress. Please Respect My Quiet.

"Mom!" Posy said. "The Fallons know you took the money. The last time I saw Wes he said it was up to his brother whether or not to call the police. Do you agree with me that it is time for you to show up and start dealing with this right now?" She practically shouted the last two words. She hadn't realized until just then how angry she was with her mom.

She liked Wes. She really, really liked Wes and whatever might have happened between them had been doomed from the start because of her mother.

"Don't shout, Posy. You always get so dramatic."

"I'm not being dramatic, Mom. You're in danger of going to jail, in the worst case, and having your crimes revealed to the entire community, in the best case. Don't you think that's a fairly serious situation?"

"I never meant to hurt anyone," Trish said.

Posy leaned against the spare room's sole piece of furniture besides the bed—a desk—and crossed her arms. "But you have hurt people. I had to take out a loan to pay the money back. The Hand-to-Hand project is just getting off the ground. What will their donors do if they find out the bank account was plundered?"

"Posy, stop shouting at me. People can hear you!"

"Stop trying to shame me!" Posy shouted. "I'm sick of it."

Her mom's eyes widened for real that time. Posy had never said anything like that to her mother. Even when she chose to live with her dad, she never told her mom why. Never said that Trish made her feel out of step every minute of every day. Even when her mom tried to be supportive, she sometimes wound up cutting Posy down, like when she gave helpful suggestions about choosing pastel clothing so she would fade just a bit. Apparently, full force, Posy was too much for some people.

"I was not trying to shame you," Trish said. "I was merely pointing out—"

"That I'm too loud. I know it. I'm too loud. I dress in bright colors. I try too hard. It's not feminine. People don't like it." Posy was shaking. "I know it all, Mom, because you've told me all those things as long as I can remember. The problem is, this is me. I can't change who I am. All I can do is try to be the best person I can. And what that means for me, right now, is to sell your inventory and your collections and try to recoup as much money as we can so you can start fresh with the surgeon in Ohio."

"I think you should go, Posy. Come back when you're ready to speak in a civilized way."

"I'll go. But I want to know. Should I go all the way to Rochester, back to my condo and my job? Or should I just go back to your house and your mess and your dog who should never have been named Angel?" Posy wanted to poke her mom, to wake her up. "Or maybe I should go right to the community center and find Wes and his brother and ask if they want to send my mom to jail."

Her mother sat on the bed and folded her hands. It didn't matter what Posy said to her, Trish pointed to the silent-retreat card on the wall.

She left, more angry than she'd ever been.

"I'VE NEVER SLEPT with a woman and not called her the next day." Wes held the phone close to his mouth. He wasn't exactly whispering, but he was trying to stay quiet. "Not even that time I accidentally made out with my date's twin sister. I called *both* of them the next day."

His old college roommate, Oliver, snorted in disgust. "And then you invited them to join us at the diner for breakfast and they actually showed up."

Wes slumped lower in the driver's seat of his truck parked outside Posy's house. He didn't want her to see him. Not just yet.

"Exactly."

Just because their lawyer was trying to figure out if they'd have to press charges against Posy's mom was no reason for him to break his streak of gentlemanly phone calls the next day. Or maybe it was the perfect reason, but he didn't want to break his streak. Last night, the part before her confession had been something outside his experience.

"You're not even giving me a challenge, Wes," Oliver said. "She's got profiles set up all over the main social media sites."

He lifted his head half an inch and took another look at Posy's house.

"Well, can you tell if the stuff she told me is true? She works for the Hotel Marie? Lives in Rochester? Any basketball stats?"

"I feel like a stalker," Oliver said. "Why are you whispering?"

"I'm not," Wes whispered.

"Please tell me you're not crouched under her bedroom window," Oliver said.

Wes banged his fist on his knee. The thing about Oliver was, he wasn't very adept at actually cultivating relationships with other people, but he was shockingly perceptive. Couple that with his abundant smarts and you got a guy who was practically impervious to misdirection.

Wes liked him precisely because Oliver had no secret layers, no hidden agendas, no capacity for or interest in lying. On the other hand, Oliver didn't shy away from awkward questions and he was the first one to call bullshit when he saw it.

"Of course not," Wes said. "I'm in my truck."

"Parked outside her house, on the phone with me, trying to find out if she's lying to you." Oliver made the disgusted noise again. Wes almost asked him if he needed an antibiotic for his cough. "Get out and knock on the door, Wes."

"I will," Wes whispered. "As soon as you tell me what you found out."

"You could have looked this up yourself, you know.

Is there something you want to talk about? Is that why you're really calling me?"

Wes considered hanging up, but in addition to being perceptive and smart, Oliver had a memory that wouldn't quit. He'd just pick this conversation up in exactly the same spot the next time they talked.

"I... Can you just... I don't know. I'll call you later. After you tell me what you know."

"This is creepy. Sitting outside her house, looking her up on the internet."

"*I'm* not looking her up. You are. And creepy would be if I had a telescope."

"No, creepy would be you sitting outside instead of going up and ringing the bell. You slept with her. I think you should be able to ask her a couple questions."

A little kid rolled past on her scooter followed by a smaller kid on a plastic motorcycle and a woman who must be their mom. The woman noticed him inside the truck and he saw her glance at the front bumper as she went by. Memorizing the license plate, no doubt, so she could report the creepy guy stalking Posy Jones.

"It's only creepy if she catches me," Wes said. "So hurry up."

Oliver was silent for a few seconds. This was taking too long. "Didn't you patent a search algorithm and sell it for a small fortune?" Wes snapped.

"I thought if I stalled long enough you would tell me you didn't care what I found because you realized there's no way you can ever get a guarantee that the woman you're dating isn't lying to you."

It was Wes's turn to snort.

"You were waiting for me to tell you that?"

"I suppose you could have said, 'Screw this, your search is taking too long. I'm going in.' But the sentiment would have been the same."

"She already lied to me, Oliver."

"I know it. She knows it. You know it. Now make up your mind what you think about that. Can you have a relationship with her if she lied to you about her mom? Do you want a relationship? If not, why are you sitting outside her house asking me to stalk her on the internet?"

Wes didn't have an answer for that one. He must have been silent so long that Oliver lost patience. His friend finally said, "She's telling the truth about her job, and I give her my seal of approval based on her privacy protection standards." He waited a beat and then said, "And a second seal of approval based on this picture of her accepting an award from the National Hospitality Organization. She has excellent legs."

Wes hadn't seen her legs since late last night. He missed her legs. He hadn't realized how much before Oliver mentioned them.

"I have a perfect record," Wes said. "I always call the next day."

"Then call. Or go knock on the door. You didn't drive away, did you?"

"No."

"Go before she sees you," Oliver said. "No woman who locks her Facebook down is going to date a stalker."

"Lucky thing she didn't catch me, then."

He hung up and got out of his truck. When he started up the walk, Posy opened the front door and squinted at him. "Wes?" She shaded her eyes with her hand. "Were you watching my house?"

Busted.

"I got a call right when I pulled up." He had no idea how to start this conversation. He didn't even know what conversation he wanted to have. "I like your house." The flower beds beside her front door were in need of attention, but everything else about the white, standard-issue split-level ranch house was neat, suburban. There was even a wreath on the front door.

"It's my mom's." She folded her arms across her middle. She was wearing those navy track pants again and had her hair pulled back in a thick ponytail. That hair had been spread on his pillows less than eight hours ago.

"Right. I forgot." Now that she'd mentioned her mom, he was even less sure what to say. There was a small pile of what looked like dog biscuits on the walkway and a trail of biscuits leading up the steps to the front door. "Is Snoopy coming over for a picnic?"

"I'm trying to trap a dog."

"This is a dog trap?"

"For a wild schnoodle."

She pointed across the street and he saw something white crouched in the dark cave created by two big bushes near the corner of a blue ranch house.

"A schnoodle?"

"Poodle-schnauzer mix," she explained. "My mother's dog has answered the call of the wild. Next thing I know, she'll be bringing coyote pals over to play Xbox or inviting a pack of wolves home for Sunday dinner."

The schnoodle emerged fully from the bushes just as he turned to get a better look at her.

Small. White. Fluffy.

What the hell?

He stared at the dog until she flicked her tail and took off running around the side of the house.

"Angel!" Posy shouted. "Come!"

Angel?

"That's your dog?" he asked.

"My mother's dog. I don't live here, remember?"

Right. She didn't live here. And that was definitely not the same dog he'd seen on the street in Madrid.

He touched the scar behind his ear.

The dog he'd see in Madrid had been a Spanish dog. A real, living breathing dog that just happened to be the doppelgänger of Posy's wild poodle. Schnoodle.

Angel.

"How long has she had that dog?" he asked.

She'd been staring across the street in the direction her mom's dog took, but now her attention snapped back to him. Her eyebrows were so expressive. He could almost read her thoughts. Right now she was trying to figure out what the hell he was up to.

"A few years, why?"

"No reason," he answered. He was not going to tell her about the doppelgänger. "I'm thinking about getting a dog."

"I'll give you one," Posy said. "You just need a net. Or a bear trap."

"Won't she come home when she's hungry?"

"She does come home. She comes home, eats the food in her bowl and waits for any chance to escape again. I had her corralled in the house, but these guys came over to pack up some of my mom's stuff and one of them held the door open and she was gone again." Posy sighed. "I should stop feeding her. I just—"

"Don't want her to go hungry?"

"If you tell her, I'll kill you." Posy looked at him. "Wes, what are you doing here?"

"I talked to Deacon. He's getting in touch with a lawyer. He doesn't want to press charges. He's going to do what he can to make sure your mom doesn't get in trouble."

Posy took a deep breath. "Thank you."

"Thank *you*," Wes said. "You're the one who paid the money back. Julia asked me where you got it and I realized I didn't even ask you."

"That would be impolite."

"I was too busy yelling at you." Wes put his hands in the pockets of his jeans at the memory of how mad he'd been. How he hadn't done anything to pull back his anger. He'd wanted her to know he was furious. "I'm sorry about that. You didn't deserve it. You were just cleaning up after your mom."

She squinted across the street, one hand shading her eyes.

"Where did you get the money?"

"Wes, this is a very uncomfortable subject for me."

"I know you said you're selling your mom's house and closing the store, but you didn't get the money from those yet and you wrote an awfully big check yesterday." Her hand *had* been shaking when she gave it to him. "Let me help, Posy. I can pay the money back."

"No!" Her eyes flashed to his face. "No. Absolutely not."

"Posy, come on. It's no problem." He wouldn't even miss the money. "Let me."

"No," she said again, forcefully. "Wes, when I was covering up what my mom did, I felt awful. I wanted to tell you. Then we slept together and I couldn't keep it a secret anymore. Now the secret is out and your brother has the money and none of that is between us anymore."

He took a step toward her, keeping his hands in his pockets. "What is between us now?"

"I don't know," Posy said.

"What do you want?"

"Wes, maybe it's better if we—"

"No," he said quickly. He didn't want her to finish her thought. She was so strong, if she decided something, he wasn't sure he'd be able to change her mind. "It's not better."

Neither of them said anything for a few seconds.

"Maybe it's better if we start over." He looked around the yard, taking in the house, the wreath, the trail of dog biscuits. "I'm Wes," he said. "I just moved to town and I'm thinking about getting a dog. I always wanted one."

She shook her head, the end of her ponytail sliding

across her shoulders. "Wes, this is dumb. We can't just ignore everything else."

"Tell me what it's like to have a dog."

She hesitated. He was afraid she was going to walk away. Instead, she cleared her throat and said, "I don't know what it's like to have a dog. Angel is more a spawn of the devil. You didn't have a dog when you were a kid?"

"No. I always wanted one, though."

"What kind of dog are you going to get?" She held up a hand. "Wait, let me guess. Stand still."

Was this really going to work? Could they get past last night and see what came next?

"You can't guess something like that just by look-ing at a person."

"This is what I do for a living," she said. "Let me get a good look."

"You do not assess human–dog compatibility for a living."

POSY HAD NO IDEA how he'd convinced her to stay here, to keep talking. It was rare for her to feel comfortable with herself when she was in Kirkland, but yesterday she'd been that comfortable with Wes. So when he was there, outside her mom's house, offering to talk to her even though he had every right to hate her and her mom, she couldn't turn him away.

"One of my roles is location scout for Hotel Marie. I visit neighborhoods and cities and determine if they are suitable for the clientele we want to attract. You can tell a lot about a place based on the kind of dogs people have there."

"I'm not that easy to read," he said.

"Then why won't you stand still and let me have a look."

Her control slipped and some of the need she'd been feeling ever since he got out of his truck slipped through in her voice.

He faced her. He took his hands out of his pockets and held his arms slightly away from his body.

She didn't move toward him, but when he opened himself up to her, leaving himself vulnerable in front of her, she felt the distance between them close just the same. It wasn't scientifically possible that the day got twenty degrees warmer, but there was heat between them just the same.

He shifted his feet. "You don't look like a schnoodle type of person," he said.

"My mom looks exactly like a schnoodle person."

She took her time looking him over, from his buzzed hair, to the dark shadow of beard on his face, to the black V-neck T-shirt that clung to his chest, and then straight down his long, strong legs in slim-cut Levi's to his beat-up black boots.

She'd been with him last night, her hands on his skin, his hands on her. They'd moved together and she'd felt every line and angle of his body. There was nothing under his clothes she hadn't seen and touched. He was strong and competitive and wanted just as hard as she did.

He needed a dog who could keep up with him, some breed that was big enough to wrestle with him and had a personality he couldn't dominate. He'd been hurt when he was a kid. Loyalty mattered to him. Trust.

She knew which dog she was going to recommend, but he was right there in front of her and God help her, she was shallow. Later maybe she'd call Maddy and confess to objectifying the perfectly nice guy in front of her, but for now she gave him another once-over, this time starting with his boots and then riding his lean strength right back up to his eyes.

He bent one elbow and flexed. "Seen enough?" Pivoting, he switched arms.

"More than enough. Put your arm down."

If he hadn't been laughing, she'd have wanted to kick him for being obnoxious, but even though Wes knew how good-looking he was, he didn't use his gifts as a weapon. She might have atoned for her lying when she washed the chapel floor, but she was in trouble all over again, this time for lust.

"Well? What's the perfect dog for me? I can't wait to hear this."

He was still smirking because he honestly believed she couldn't see him for who he was. Straight up, straightforward. Steady and true.

"German shepherd."

He did a double take and she knew she'd pegged him right.

"Lucky guess."

She nodded. Except it hadn't been a guess. He had

Rin Tin Tin written all over him. He'd fit right in here in Kirkland.

A low engine rumble distracted her as a van from the Kirkland Animal Patrol pulled into the driveway. The guy who was driving introduced himself as Travis.

"You the pet owners?" he asked.

"What pet?" Posy asked, although she had a bad feeling she knew exactly why Travis was there.

"Someone called in a report that there's a dog running loose in the neighborhood. Causing property damage. Gave us this address for the owners." He pulled a tablet computer out of his pocket and turned the screen to face her. "See there? They sent this picture."

In the photo, Angel was shown from the side, running away from the scene of a crime, a magazine flapping open in her jaws.

"The caller said that was the magazine out of her Sunday *New York Times.*"

Posy didn't actually need that piece of information. She'd cleaned the shredded magazine pages off the back deck that morning. The crossword puzzle had been mostly intact and she'd noticed that whoever filled it out had gotten twenty-three down incorrect.

"So," Travis said, "you the owners of that dog?"

"She is," Wes said.

At the same time Posy said, "My mother is…. Angel belongs to my mother," Posy added firmly. "My mother is away and I'm dog-sitting."

"I don't suppose the dog is properly contained inside the house at this moment?"

"No."

"Maybe she's being walked on her leash?"

Posy knew the guy was just doing his job, but she was completely fed up with being judged. "The last time I saw her, she was under the bushes across the road."

Travis scrutinized the yard, but Angel was long gone.

"Guess I'm going to take a look around, then." Travis had a round stomach and short legs, but he seemed keen on exercise. He pulled a long-handled net from the back of his van. Before he closed the door, he pointed into the van and said, "You sit tight."

Turning back to them, he explained, "Picked up a dog before I came your way. That's why I was late." He held the net over his shoulder. "You want to come along? Maybe she'll turn up if you call her."

"Fat chance," Posy muttered, but she followed him down the driveway. She wasn't surprised when Wes ambled along with them—he hadn't shown any interest in leaving, and why shouldn't he be witness to this additional dissolution of her life.

"You said she got out of the house, but then what?" Travis asked. "She get spooked by something?"

"What do you mean?"

"Why won't she come back? Most times, if you're not mistreating a dog and they don't get scared or hurt, they come on home when they're tired or hungry."

He used the end of the pole to lift the bottom branches of a cedar tree. He and Wes both bent to look underneath.

"She does come back," Posy said. Travis's insinuation

that Angel was staying away on purpose bothered her. "She eats her food and then she leaves again."

One time she brought me a purse stuffed with twenties.

"You said she's your dog?" Travis didn't sound as if he believed her.

"No," Posy said, more slowly this time. "She's my mother's dog. I'm house-sitting."

"Maybe she's looking for your mom," Wes suggested.

Good luck with that.

They had made a complete circuit of the neighborhood and didn't once see Angel. As they walked up the driveway to Travis's van, she said, "I think she's acting out some fantasy where she's a wild animal."

Travis snorted. "Poodles don't tend to like the wild. They're house dogs."

"She's a schnoodle, though," Wes said. "Maybe the nonpoodle part is the wild part."

Posy was starting to think that mixed in with the poodle and schnauzer DNA Angel had at least a touch of wolf. Or maybe tiger.

"Besides," Wes said, "she obviously does like the wild. Some people are like that—you think they're going to be just ordinary and then they turn out to be…"

He shifted so he wasn't looking at Travis anymore, but instead met her eyes. She stopped breathing.

"…extraordinary."

The lie, her mom's theft, it was all in their way and there was no way around that, but last night meant something to him. She didn't know why he was still there, but somehow, it was okay.

"I've got a humane trap you can try. It won't hurt her, just hold her."

Travis pulled a steel box with a mesh opening on each end out of the back of his van and handed it to her. The steel was warm from sitting in the truck in the sunny driveway, but it made her feel cold.

She gave the trap right back to Travis. "I don't think she'd fall for a trap."

Travis looked around the yard again. "Could be right. Poodles are smart. Schnauzers, too. You ever read up on dog training? Lots of times bad behavior comes from being bored." He took a business card out of his wallet and wrote the name of a website on the back. "Training a dog takes time, but it will keep her and your neighbors' property safe."

Wes was peering into the back of the van.

"This is the dog you picked up?"

"Yep. He's a mutt. Got a lot of German shepherd in him," Travis answered.

Posy edged up behind them and saw a large dog standing stock-still, staring out of a cage at them. At Wes, really.

"He's a stray?"

"Nope. I picked him up from a family. Said they couldn't keep him anymore. Sometimes we get the reason, but they didn't give me details." Travis slung the metal pole and net into the back of the van. The dog didn't flinch at the bang.

She wondered if he was deaf.

"What's his name?" Wes asked.

"Bubba."

"That is exactly the kind of dog I want," Wes said. "He looks noble, don't you think?"

Posy thought he looked as if he might be sleepwalking. Or stuffed. But she didn't say that.

"He's going to be in quarantine for a couple days and then you can come see about adoption."

Travis shut the back door of the van.

"If you catch your dog, you keep her on a leash from now on."

Posy nodded.

As the animal control van pulled out, Chloe Chastain came out of her house and crossed the street toward them. Posy recognized her right away, but Wes didn't realize who it was until she was starting up the driveway. When he did pick her out, he said, "She's your neighbor?"

"My mother's neighbor," Posy muttered.

Chloe's outfit, a turquoise-and-white sundress with a sweet white wrap sweater on top, was fresh and sunny. Posy glanced down at her own track pants and Nikes and then straightened her shoulders.

"Wes, what a surprise to see you here," Chloe said. "Or maybe not such a surprise since you're duet partners?"

Posy felt a blush run up her neck.

He tightened his lips in what might have passed for the tiniest of smiles.

Chloe tucked a piece of hair behind her ear. "Well, this is awkward, but I saw the animal control van here, so I guess you already know most of it."

"Most of what?" Posy asked.

"I called them for Angel. I had hoped to speak to your mother about this, but if she's not here…"

Posy ignored the implied question about her mother. "You called the dogcatcher on my dog?"

"I thought Angel was your mom's dog," Wes said quietly.

"Not now," she answered.

"Your mother's dog has eaten two of my rosebushes," Chloe said. "And items have gone missing from our clothesline. She also stole my paper."

Wes coughed. "We saw the photo."

"Angel ate a rosebush?" Posy asked. "Don't they have thorns?"

"Well, I don't know for certain that she ate them. She dug them up and stole them. I saw her dragging one off behind the house. Then she must have come back in the night," she said. "That's when she got the other one."

Posy was proud that she didn't smile and she didn't look over at Chloe's house. Later she'd check out the damage and gloat that Angel had mucked up their land-scaped perfection, but for now, it was important to look like a responsible citizen.

"Okay. Well, I'll write you a check to cover them…?"

Between her mom and Angel, she was going to be broke.

Chloe put her hand to her mouth. "Oh, no, Posy. I

don't want to be *paid*. I just wanted your mother to know that Angel's been up to mischief."

Of course, Posy thought. That was what people always wanted. Step out of line in this neighborhood and you were marked.

"Okay," Posy said. "Now I know."

"Well, okay," Chloe said. Posy hoped she was disappointed that she hadn't gotten more of a response.

"Hey, Chloe, I meant to ask, did you get your purse back?"

"My purse?"

"I found it on the street. Must have fallen off the roof of your car or something. I put it on the porch and then forgot to tell you."

"I can't believe I left it on the roof of the car. That's not like me."

Posy shrugged. "I wouldn't know about that."

"Thank you," Chloe said.

An awkward silence fell on them.

"Well," she said. "Good to see you, Wes. Hope things work out with your dog. Nice to see you, too, Chloe. I have a lot to do inside. So…"

She wasn't sure what to say next. She spun and walked into her mom's house.

CHLOE'S SMILE SPARKLED. He couldn't afford to antagonize her, but man, did her sparkle rub him the wrong way.

"Posy was always prickly," she said. "So difficult."

"She's had a rough couple of days."

"Well," Chloe said, "I think with me, it's more than that. We've never gotten along. Posy never wanted to do the things the rest of our group did, but her mother insisted we include her and then Posy would try to take over or she'd sabotage plans. It's just how she is."

Wes was uncomfortable having this conversation with Chloe on Posy's front walk. Actually, he was uncomfortable having this conversation anywhere with Chloe.

"Probably makes sense to keep out of each other's way, then," he said.

Chloe pursed her lips. "The problem is that I put my reputation on the line with this fundraiser. I used my network to raise a lot of money and I'm absolutely certain something happened that Trish and Posy aren't telling us." Her eyes narrowed and for the first time, Wes thought he might be seeing the real Chloe, who was both smarter and less cheery than the persona she'd been wearing. "You've never had to work for a living, have you?"

"I work," he said.

"You work, but you don't have to. Your brother could and would take care of you," she said. "He gave you the job you have now, right?"

Wes nodded.

"I married my high school sweetheart. I sold real estate for two years, but knew as soon as I got pregnant that I was going to quit and be a stay-at-home mom." She glanced over her shoulder at the house across the street. "We bought that house from my parents. When my husband left me, I almost lost the house because I couldn't make the mortgage."

"Chloe, I—"

"My blog shouldn't work. Most of them don't. It's very, very hard to make a living as a blogger, but I do it because I work harder than anyone I know. The internet is vicious, Wes." She touched his arm. "If my readers or a rival blogger or one of the hundreds of sites that make money by mocking other sites catches a whiff of impropriety about that money, I could be finished. And then my job, and my income, and the life I've made for my girls is gone faster than you can say viral. You and your brother want to have your community program here in Kirkland. You should remember who lives here and who's running back to Rochester as fast as she can."

"I'm not sure where you're going with this, Chloe," he said.

"I'm going back to my house. But if I see the slightest chance that my reputation is going to be damaged by whatever Trish got up to with that money, I'm going to the police. You might be able to afford to hope she doesn't get caught, but I can't."

"My brother has the money from the fundraiser," he said. "He has the records of the donors and our lawyer is going to double-check all the documentation, starting today."

"That's great, Wes," Chloe said. "I'm glad you guys got your money. But Posy wrote that check and you and I both know she shouldn't have had to. There was a fundraising account and that's not where the money came from."

She went back to her house and Wes let her get a head start before he walked to his truck. The threat was clear and, God help him, he could understand where she was coming from. He was going to have to talk to Deacon again. As much as he wanted to discount Chloe, she had a point. She'd gone out of her way to raise money for their project and they couldn't leave her dangling in the wind. He just wished there was some way to protect Chloe's reputation that didn't involve turning Posy's mom in to the police.

He was about to open the door to his truck when he noticed the dog. He didn't see where she came from but there she was, sitting in the grass a few feet away from him. He didn't want to spook her, so he lowered himself carefully to one knee and held a hand out.

"Hey, Angel," he said.

The dog cocked her head. She had one ear that flopped forward like a regular dog and the other stuck straight out from her head. The stuck-out ear twitched when he talked to her, circling the air as if looking for better reception. "You ever been to Madrid?"

She gave one sharp bark and then took off across Posy's lawn and disappeared under the neighbor's shed. He thought he saw Posy inside her mom's house and looked up, but the window was empty. He shook his head. He needed to talk to Deacon.

AFTER HIS TRUCK PULLED AWAY, Posy peeked out from behind her mom's brocade drapes and surveyed Chloe's yard. Now that she knew to look, the messy holes were obvious, one beside the mailbox at the end of the driveway and the other right next to the front steps.

She went into the kitchen and dug out the box of dog biscuits. The instructions said a dog Angel's size should have no more than two a day. Opening the sliding glass door, she lined three biscuits up on the porch. Two was enough for domesticated dogs, but Angel was wild now. She probably needed more calories for all her landscaping work. She spotted Angel crouched under the Nickersons' shed. Posy pointed at the biscuits and said, "Dessert. No strings attached."

CHAPTER FOURTEEN

"WHERE ARE YOU?" Deacon asked into the phone. "Is that barking?"

"I'm at the animal shelter," Wes said. "I'm getting a dog."

"You're getting a dog?" Wes heard a rustling and then Deacon's muffled voice shouting to Julia, "He's getting a dog!"

Bubba would be in quarantine for another week, but they'd let him sign the papers that morning. As long as Bubba didn't develop a disease or bite anyone before his time was up, Wes would be allowed to take him home. The shelter had a small, fenced exercise area and he'd taken Bubba out there to get to know him.

The dog had been sitting up in the grass next to Wes's legs, but his front legs slid gradually out until he flopped onto his side. The woman at the desk had said there might be an adjustment period when Bubba felt anxious around Wes because he'd had so much change in his life. If this was anxiety, Wes wondered what relaxed would look like. He scratched Bubba's ears and the dog's eyes closed.

"Why are you so excited about the dog?" Wes asked.

"No reason," Deacon said. "Just happy you're settling down."

Just happy you're probably not going to walk in front of a truck again today. He needed Deacon to let that go.

"I called you because I'm worried about Chloe Chastain."

He told his brother about the conversation he'd had with Chloe the day before. The shelter was a few miles outside Kirkland. When he turned onto Main Street earlier that morning, the sun was in his face and lit the street, making it look even more like a movie set than ever. It reminded him of something Posy had said: "Don't believe everything you hear." That was true about Kirkland and about a lot of other things.

"As much as I don't want to see her point, I do," Wes said. "Her reputation is on the line just as much as the Fallon Foundation's."

"So what should we do?"

He'd brought a tennis ball with him and he bounced it off the cinder-block wall of the shelter and caught it in one hand. The irony of having this conversation about jail while he was locked in a small chain-link pen was not lost on him.

"I'm supposed to say that we need to press charges against Trish," he said. "But she's Posy's mom. I just—"

He sat on the grass with his hand on Bubba's head. The dog sighed and stretched his neck so his nose was buried against Wes's hip.

Moms weren't something he and Deacon talked

about much. He didn't remember anything about their mother—he'd been barely two years old when she died in a fire at a nightclub on a night when she'd called in sick to work. There'd been a time when he pressured Deacon to tell him stories, to share his memories, but he'd realized after a while that Deacon wasn't keeping the stories from him. There weren't any stories.

Their mom had been too young, too caught up in her troubled marriage, too selfish. And toward the end of her life, too broken to really be a mother.

"What?"

"I know they don't have the best relationship. There's friction. But they're hanging on to each other somehow. Am I really going to have her mom arrested?"

"I don't like it any more than you do, but we might not have a choice. Vic's supposed to call later today. I'll get him to conference the lawyer in and see where things stand."

Wes hung up and then threw the ball against the wall again. Bubba's ears twitched but he didn't move. The shelter didn't know why the previous owners had surrendered the dog. The woman at the desk told him that usually when the owners wouldn't give a reason that meant there was a behavior problem.

He dropped the ball and scratched deep under Bubba's chin, digging into the thick ruff around his neck. "They must have been a pack of idiots to give up on a guy like you." Bubba rolled onto his back. "That's right. You relax. We're going to figure this out."

HE TOOK BUBBA BACK INSIDE and then went home for a quick shower before the meeting he had that afternoon with Hamilton Crane, the president of the Teaching and Interaction Center at Robinson University. Hamilton held the purse strings for the grant they wanted for the Hand-to-Hand centers.

He'd expected that a guy with a name like Hamilton would be stuffy or at the least formal, but he adjusted his expectations fast when he walked into Hamilton's office and was faced with a thickly muscled guy juggling three apples and a cantaloupe. A college-age girl with her hair in low ponytails under a newsboy cap held a flip camera on the guy as she circled him.

"Wes Fallon, right?" the juggler asked.

"Right."

"Hamilton Crane. Lauren is almost finished. I'll be right with you."

"Stop talking," Lauren said. "I can edit sound out, but your lips will still be moving."

Hamilton reversed the direction of the juggling and then tossed each piece of fruit to Wes, ending with the cantaloupe. Lauren closed the camera, and Wes clapped as she excused herself.

"Thanks," Hamilton said. "It's for a video Lauren is making for her math tutorial."

Hamilton's private office had a wall of windows facing out into the main room of the center where clusters of computers and white boards were grouped with low seating, creating mobile, agile classroom spaces.

"So, Wes, we're impressed with the work the Fallon

centers do, but as I told your brother, we want to be sure it's the right fit for our resources. Deacon said you can tell us more about the impact of the centers." Hamilton took a bottle of water out of a small fridge next to his desk and passed it to Wes before opening one for himself. "You're the ambassador. So let's hear it."

Wes was ready. He'd memorized the statistics and he had a brochure, an annual report and a book of case studies all set to give to Hamilton. As he passed each one over, he could see Hamilton's interest wavering. He'd probably seen literature exactly like that a million times.

Wes stood and said, "My brother built the first center in our hometown. I was eighteen, cocky, lost, stupid and about to get kicked off my college team and probably out of school. Deacon didn't know how to help me. He took me back to Milton where we coached the girls basketball team." He leaned over and flipped the case-study book to the back page. "That's them, right there."

Hamilton nodded. "I knew about the team, but not the part about you."

"When we went there, Deacon was trying to fix me. He thought if I saw what life looked like for people without my advantages, I'd go back to school and settle down."

That had been the winter when Deacon met Julia and almost lost her because he was too proud to admit he couldn't read. And Wes almost lost his chance at playing college ball because he was too afraid to tell Deacon he felt like a failure. Nothing had been working until they were honest with each other.

"And did it work?" Hamilton raised the bottle of water. "Did you go back to school and settle down?"

"Going back there was the best thing we ever did. By the time the season was over, it had changed our lives. People look at places like Milton—no jobs, no stability, no culture, none of the stuff you've got on Main Street here in Kirkland—and they see a place with nothing to offer. My brother looks at towns like Milton and Kirkland and sees all the ways they can help each other."

Wes gestured through the window to the common area.

"You've got all these resources here, and I've seen your results. The tutoring services you offer are top-notch. Deacon's vision is the same as it's been since we spent that season in Milton. Everybody has something to offer and everybody needs a hand sometimes. You give us a hand, partner with us to provide these remote-tutoring resources, and I guarantee your life is going to be changed. You'll never look back."

Hamilton stood and shook his hand. "Your brother knows how to pick his ambassadors," he said. "Tell Deacon I'll call him tomorrow afternoon."

"Call him with a yes?"

"My board is meeting in the morning. If I have anything to say about the decision, it will be a yes. For sure."

He waited until he was in the parking structure before he let himself yell. He'd done it.

He wanted to celebrate.

He wanted to see Posy.

WITH THE COLLECTIONS gone from the house, Posy had interviewed several Realtors and made her choice. Sandy, the woman she picked, was relatively new to Kirkland. There was a slight chance she might miss out on some potential buyers because she wasn't as well connected as the more established brokers, but on the other hand, she was far less likely to gossip about Posy and Trish in the course of the sale.

Sandy took the signed contracts with her and left a list of suggestions for improvements Posy might want to make to maximize the house's appeal. Posy was in the basement, sorting through her mom's clutter when the doorbell rang.

Angel zipped up the stairs and stuck her nose in the crack under the door, her tail wagging fast. Posy looked out the window and saw Wes's tall frame silhouetted by the porch light.

He had a white take-out bag in his left hand and was balancing a six-pack of Coke and a bakery box in his right. He didn't notice that she was at the window, so she let herself look a bit longer than was necessary. Angel panted at the door and Posy thought she knew exactly how the dog felt. She wanted more of Wes. As much as she could get.

She picked the dog up and clamped one firm hand on her collar. "You're not getting out tonight," she said as she opened the door. "The dogcatcher's coming for you if you're not careful."

"I don't think Travis would like to be called a dogcatcher, Posy."

"Hi," she said.

He smiled. "I brought sandwiches and cheesecake from the Lemon Drop. Can I bribe my way in for dinner?"

She stepped back and held the door. "I'm cleaning the basement. If you'd called—"

"If I'd called you'd have had a chance to explain why we shouldn't have dinner together and I didn't want to give you that chance. I got good news today about the Hand-to-Hand program and I want to celebrate." He tilted his head toward her. "With you."

She didn't think he did that head-tilting thing on purpose, but good Lord, it made her knees weak. She closed the door and flipped the lock before putting Angel down, but the dog hadn't shown the slightest interest in escape. Instead, she sniffed Wes's shoes and the bottoms of his jeans.

"I was at the shelter," he said. "I've adopted Bubba."

It took her a second to remember the big shepherd mutt from Travis's van. "Congratulations."

She should be happy for both of them, she knew, but the dog seemed like just one more root he was digging into the soil of Kirkland. Before he knew it, Wes would be as much a piece of the town as the Lemon Drop. The one place in the world she was least herself.

She led him up the few stairs into the living room.

The curtains were wide open and the late-evening sun streamed in, making the creamy woodwork and newly polished floors shine.

"Your mom's place is beautiful," Wes said. "It's different than the store, though. I thought there'd be more… stuff."

"There was. I'm clearing it out so we can put it on the market." She ran her hands down the sides of her jeans. "Um, I'm really busy. You wouldn't believe how much work this is and I have to get back to my job tomorrow. So I—"

"I'll help," Wes said.

"What? Help?"

"Yeah. I don't have anything to do. Come on, I'm strong. Put me to work." He tried to pose, flexing the biceps on the side where he was balancing the bakery box, but the box slid forward and started toward the floor.

She jumped and grabbed the box, righting it quickly. She ended up closer to him than she'd meant to be, and his gaze met hers.

"I don't know what we're doing, Posy."

She shut her eyes.

"Let me help."

She couldn't tell him to go.

CHAPTER FIFTEEN

IF HE'D BEEN SURPRISED at the clear spaces upstairs, he recognized the basement as the work of the same collector who'd put together Wonders. Boxes were stacked from floor to ceiling around all four sides of the large space. A big garbage can rested next to a table covered with packing tape, markers and strips of colored dot stickers. Posy seemed to have been using that area as a command center.

Posy devoured her roast-beef sandwich and then apologized. "I didn't stop for lunch," she said. "I had a fantasy that I was going to get through the basement before I went to bed tonight."

He put the second half of his sandwich down and wiped his mouth on a paper napkin. "So let's do it. Show me what you need."

The boxes stacked near the stairs all had to be moved to the garage, so they spent the next half hour shuffling up and down the basement stairs. He had two cartons of books balanced in his arms when Posy started down the stairs toward him. He turned to face the wall and she slid behind him, one of her hips brushing across the back of his jeans. He was grateful she couldn't see the effect that touch had on him.

When they'd finished that, Posy got glasses of water from the kitchen and they ate cheesecake from the paper containers. She boosted herself up to sit on a steamer trunk and he settled on the floor in front of her.

The wall behind her was lined with plastic tubs labeled with her name. Posy—age 8. Posy—artwork, elementary. Posy—sophomore.

"What's with all the boxes?" He gestured with his fork.

She blushed pink. "My mom is a collector," she said. "She never threw anything out."

"When you sell the house, what happens to all that?"

"I'm getting rid of it. Those boxes we just put in the garage are for the Goodwill. The guys are coming tomorrow. I'm getting a Dumpster delivered for this and the ones I stacked near the stairs. That will leave just—"

"You're throwing all this away?" he interrupted her, putting his plate down and walking over to the bins. He ran a hand over the outside of the stack. There must have been close to fifteen of them, all full of Posy's childhood. Her mother had cared enough to save and sort and store all this for her.

"I told my mom she had two choices, come home and help or let me make the decisions. She's not here, so it's all going out the door."

He was tempted to crack open a tub and look inside. Just to see what kind of things her mom had kept, what kind of things Posy didn't see a need to even sort through before she threw them away.

She set her plate down and joined him.

"Don't you want to look? Maybe keep some of it for yourself? For your kids?"

Posy shook her head. "I know how it seems. Like I'm throwing this out to spite my mom." She kicked the bottom of the tub in front of them. "But that's not me inside there. It's my mom's story of me. Who she wanted me to be and who I hardly ever was." She pointed to a tub labeled Posy—dance. "See that one? She made me take dance lessons right along with Chloe and all the other little girlie girls in my class. I was awful. One year at the recital, I was doing a jump and I overshot my mark. I landed practically on top of the piano player and broke his wrist. I was so mortified, but I thought at least I wouldn't have to dance anymore." She touched the tub again. "Wrong. She made me go right back to lessons the next week."

Wes put his hand on her shoulder. "That's a terrible story."

"I don't need this, Wes," she said. "When it's all gone, my mom might still have compulsive issues, but without the house or the store, they won't be as bad. She'll be able to manage without me. I'll be free."

He leaned down to kiss her. He didn't understand how things got so wrong between her and her mom, but he wanted her to know he was there. That he heard her, even if he didn't understand.

POSY LEANED INTO HIM, letting his arms and chest support her. His hands skimmed down her back and she pressed closer to him, to the support of his frame.

She wanted to believe Wes understood but she doubted he could.

She looped her fingers into his waistband just above his hip bone, letting her fingers slide down between the fabric and his skin. He moaned against her mouth and she pressed her palm flat, sliding her hand from his hip around to the front of his jeans where his erection pressed against his zipper.

His hands dipped inside the V-neck of her shirt, his long fingers sliding under her bra to touch the sensitive skin of her breast. His touch jolted her and she moved against him, more insistent, wanting more than he was giving.

When he moved his hand, she missed the contact even though their mouths were still joined and her hands were on him. And then he was cupping his hands under her and lifting, spinning them, holding her tight against him.

She'd known he was strong, but hadn't expected this. He pulled her tight against him and then his lips moved from her mouth to her jaw, to trail down her neck. She lifted her head to give him better access to the places he was so skillfully attending to and glanced across at the tubs.

Reality slammed into her.

She put her hands on his shoulders and pushed backward, forcing him to let her slide down.

"I can't do this here. Not with Mom's storage all around me."

"Okay, then where? Upstairs?"

She shook her head. He didn't understand. Kirkland made her nuts. She wanted to be with him in her real life, not here, where everything she was working to remove from her life pressed in tight.

"I have to go back to work tomorrow for a few days. I'm doing an inspection at our hotel in Niagara Falls. Come with me."

"Take Your Lover To Work Day?"

"My boss doesn't mind if I travel with someone else on the inspections. It helps with the cover story, actually. We can have two nights away from here for ourselves."

He hesitated. "I don't know if I should go away right now. We're close—"

"Please come with me," she said. "I want you to."

"Two days. We have to be back in two days."

"No problem."

He nodded.

They went back upstairs together and he convinced her that a good-night kiss was necessary. That led to a little more than a kiss, but he finally went back to his apartment, leaving her alone with Angel.

She slept in the guest bedroom again, her dreams full of Wes and a hotel room far from Kirkland.

MADDY WAS BEHIND the Guest Services desk when Posy came in. She handed her a set of house keys and Angel's feeding and walk schedule. Posy had told her not to worry if Angel got out, but she hoped Angel wouldn't escape. She'd only be gone two days. Making these plans for Angel made it clear that she was going to have to do something about the dog if her mom wasn't going to take her back. She remembered Travis with his net and his trap and then how funny Angel looked when she jumped from the arm of the couch to fling herself on Posy whenever she came home.

She didn't have to sort the dog out yet.

"Hey," Posy said, "do you know where my mom is?"

Her cousin carefully smoothed the shiny wood surface of the desk. "I do, but she doesn't want to receive visitors."

"Well, maybe you can pretend to forget that just long enough to tell me where she is."

"I can't," Maddy said. "Our hospitality rules forbid it."

"She's taking advantage of you," Posy said. "She's taking advantage of you and putting you in the middle. Don't let her do that to you."

"She's been genuinely upset," Maddy explained. "The surgeon was out of the country for a week or so and she hasn't been able to get in touch with him. I think she's worried he's dumped her."

"It's entirely possible he never existed in the first place, you know?" Posy rolled her eyes. "I don't want her putting all her eggs in his basket, anyway. She needs to look for an apartment here in Kirkland, one that allows pets!"

"Okay. Her house isn't going to sell that fast. We have time to work on this."

"Can I write her a note?"

Maddy passed her a sheet of paper and a pen.

Dear Mom,
Angel's fine, thanks for asking. I heard the surgeon
is playing hard to get. You should think about
doing that, too. Why don't you come home, help
me deal with Wonders, and then we'll rent a place
for you downtown. You don't want to stay silent
forever, do you?
Your daughter,
Posy

She thought she'd be able to calm down before she picked Wes up, but the anger stayed with her, coiled right under her skin.

It wasn't about the fundraiser or even about being left holding the bag with the house and the store. No, she was furious with her mom for hiding behind Maddy. The number of decent relationships she had in Kirkland was small. Why did her mom have to take her issues and store them at Maddy's retreat house?

She'd told Wes she'd pick him up at his office, so she parked in a visitor's spot and went inside the town hall. She was a few steps before the conference room near the mayor's office when she heard a burst of laughter. Curious, she glanced in as she was about to go by. She stopped when she saw Wes at the front of the room in the center of a small knot of men. The mayor was there and his assistant. A few of the others she recognized from the town board. She watched as they listened to Wes and then laughed again.

Wes's face was lit up, from the spark in his eyes to

the sexy twist at the corners of his mouth. She knew exactly why those guys were hanging on his stories. He was magnetic.

Being able to pull people in, make them feel special, read them and give them back what they wanted was a gift. Wes had that gift in spades.

She ducked back around the corner of the doorway and waited until the meeting broke up. Wes walked through the door with the mayor on one side and his assistant on the other. "Posy!" he said. "I'll be there in one minute."

She nodded and went outside to wait for him at her car.

Seeing Wes in his element had inflamed her anger. With all his gifts and all his strengths, there must be a thousand and one jobs he could do, and do well. Why should he be stuck here in Kirkland, doing his brother's flunky work? He deserved the chance to discover his own life.

She'd worked up a decent head of steam by the time he came out. He had a leather duffel over one shoulder and a blue fleece in his hand. Seeing him walk toward her car, knowing he was packed and ready to spend two days with her... His swagger and the light in his eyes when he waved to her... All of a sudden, the anger she'd been feeling turned to lust.

SHE GOT A SPEEDING TICKET halfway to Niagara Falls. Wes tried to switch seats with her but she wouldn't give up the wheel. Getting out of Kirkland had never felt as good as it did that day, with Wes along for the ride.

They were about ten minutes from the hotel when she said, "This is an unannounced visit. I mentioned that, right?"

He nodded.

"So we're undercover."

"Fake-mustaches undercover or just not flashing our employee ID undercover?"

"I don't think I'd remain unnoticed long if I were wearing a fake mustache."

"So I'll wear the fake mustache and you can use the fake accent." He leaned against the door, turning his shoulders to see her better. "How's your French?"

"I'm much better with Transylvanian," she said. Then she added in her best vampire-inflected tones, "Very nice to meet you, my dear."

"Oh, that's perfect. No one will ever suspect you're not an actual Transylvanian. Bravo, Posy."

"What I started to explain, Wes, is that on these inspection visits, it's important for me to assess all the amenities. I hope you won't mind."

THE EXTENDED-STAY SUITES at the Hotel Marie in Niagara Falls had hot tubs in the room. Wes dropped his duffel on the floor and took in the view from the sweeping windows, out over the town and the falls beyond. Then he turned back to the hot tub bubbling in the corner of the room opposite the fireplace.

"When you told me we had to assess all the amenities, did you know the room had a hot tub?"

Posy nodded. "Guilty."

"You're a tease," Wes said.

"Guilty again."

She pulled the thin white sheer over the window to give them privacy without blocking the light. Then she was in his arms and before long they had stripped off their clothes and were inspecting the hot tub. The jets were all in working order and the temperature was perfect.

He wanted to stay in the tub forever. The bubbling water covered Posy, naked and eager in his lap. But before he was really ready, he found that he couldn't wait.

They laid towels on the rug in front of the fireplace and made love. This time there was no hesitation. They made the most of the excellent amenities in their suite.

For the next two days, they were absorbed in each other. Posy completed her inspections, making surreptitious notes on her iPad and snapping pictures with her phone. Sometimes she made him pose in front of whatever she was really photographing. He didn't mind. It gave him an opportunity to flex for her and he knew she got a kick out of that.

He saw a new side of Posy. She was as smart and competent as ever, but she laughed more easily and the armor she wrapped around herself in Kirkland was gone. She didn't look for insults. He loved seeing her relax, but the contrast with the way she could be in Kirkland was jarring.

She seemed unable to fit in when she was in Kirkland, but seeing her at the hotel, he realized it wasn't that she couldn't fit in in Kirkland, it was that she wouldn't.

Any hope he'd been holding on to that there might be some way he could persuade her to stay slipped away.

He savored every second of the vacation, maybe more than he would have if he'd thought they stood a chance when they got back to town.

THE NEXT WEEK on Wednesday at lunchtime, Wes's rec-league team was up by twenty points in the first quarter of the game. Jay was on his team and the mayor would not stop feeding him the ball. Wes could score at will. Well, not at will, but if he put his mind to it, he could score a lot. The problem was he was bored out of his skull. His rec-league games were rapidly becoming a bigger chore than any of the weeding he did for Mrs. Meacham.

Jay shot him another pass and Wes dribbled around, pretending that Ryan, who was attempting to guard him, was an impeccable defender. In reality, he was easy to beat if Wes cut to his left, and even easier on his right. Wes passed to Jay and prayed the guy would take the ball to the basket himself.

"You're slacking," Ryan muttered.

"Forget your daily affirmations, Ryan?" Wes said. "You're good enough, you're smart enough and, gosh darn it, you can guard the lane."

Jay yelled, "Wes!" and the ball came right back to him. *Are the mayor's arms broken or what?*

Ryan swatted at the ball and Wes was tempted to put it through Ryan's legs and take it in on a fast break, but that would be rude. And humiliating. And, Wes thought, as he passed the ball to Mickey Denoria, his other guard, it wouldn't make the game any more interesting.

He watched as Mickey put the ball up, but Ryan managed to get a hand in his face to block it cleanly.

"Nice move," he said to Ryan and ignored the glare Mickey sent his way. It *was* a nice move. Moves like that were few and far between in this league and should be celebrated.

Posy would understand.

Heck, Posy would wipe the court with these guys. He wondered what she did at lunchtime. Jay wouldn't refuse if he asked him to put her on a team. Not that she'd be there much longer, but still, he could get one more good game in. He didn't even have to play. Watching Ryan guard Posy would be entertainment enough.

He took himself out of the game, trading places with John McHale, and settling on the end of the bench. Bubba, whose adoption had gone through that morning, was lying on the pavement behind the bench. Wes had decided to bring him to work for the day and he'd spent the first hour lying on the floor in Wes's office before transferring to the court to lie in the sun. Bubba seemed to have two speeds, slow and asleep, but Wes liked to think he was enjoying the change of scenery from the shelter.

Jay yelled for him, so Wes bent to fiddle with his shoelaces. He had his head down when he heard a familiar bark from the dog park on the other side of the courts.

He swiveled on the bench. Posy and Angel were just going through the gate.

He quickly untied Bubba's leash and pulled the dog up. "I'm heading out, guys! See you next week."

His pulse kicked up faster than it had during the entire game. He wanted to be here in Kirkland for his brother, but Posy was right. The place might be charming, but it was no Madrid. Not that he wanted to live in Madrid—it was too far from home—but he wasn't sure he was cut out for this life, either. Working a desk job, shooting around with the guys at lunch and then heading home to weed his garden and drink beer on the deck.

Being away with Posy had reminded him how much he enjoyed life on the road.

Posy smiled when he came through the gate.

"Is Bubba a full-fledged member of the family now?"

"As of this morning," he said. Angel dropped a tennis ball in front of him and he picked it up. Her whole body tensed with excitement, every inch of her being focused on it. Bubba didn't seem to notice the ball.

Wes reared back and flung it. Angel streaked after it, the fur on her ears streaming backward, her tail straight, her compact body flying as she ran. Bubba yawned and stretched his front legs out, rear end in the air, tail curling, until he suddenly flopped to his belly in the grass.

"Bubba lacks Angel's enthusiasm for dog games," Wes explained.

Posy slid her foot out from under Bubba's head.

"Bubba lacks enthusiasm for just about everything, as far as I can tell."

Posy wore a yellow shirt and a gray cotton skirt printed with white circles. Underneath, her legs were bare. She bent to pick up the ball when Angel returned it and he had to swallow hard at the sight of her skirt riding up enough that a guy with an active imagination could really have fun.

It didn't escape him that he was having a lot more fun walking his dog with Posy than he'd had on the court today. Or that she was still the most interesting person he'd met in Kirkland and one of the only ones he wanted to get to know better.

He poked Bubba with his toe. "Don't you want to chase the ball, buddy? This is what dogs do at the off-leash park."

Bubba shifted onto his side, exposing his belly. Wes threw the ball again for Angel and then rubbed his foot against Bubba, who closed his eyes.

"He's not really what you expected, is he?" Posy asked.

"I never had a dog," he said. "I told you."

A pair of terriers whose owner was chatting with another woman near the gate chased Angel when she ran back to drop the ball again. Posy picked up the ball and faked a throw in one direction before tossing it in another. Angel wasn't fooled by the fake out, but the terriers were. They were a few yards away when Angel took off after the ball.

"They'll never catch her," Wes said.

"No one ever catches her."

Before they ended the game, the terriers were lying panting next to Bubba. Even Angel looked slightly droopy, although she perked up enough to snarl at a Lab who tried to take the ball she'd dropped near Bubba's face. The Lab backed off a step, but then decided Angel was too far away to stop him so he went for it again. Bubba snaked out and he snatched the ball before the Lab got close. The Lab barked, trying to engage Bubba, wondering if this was a new game, but Bubba stood, shook himself once, dropped the ball next to Angel and then looked back at Wes.

"I didn't know he was even awake," Wes muttered.

"Do you wish Bubba had more pep?"

"He is who he is," Wes said. "It's not as if I'd ever return him just because he doesn't meet my fantasy of what a perfect dog would be."

"Some people would," Posy said. "Heck, someone already did. Isn't that why he was up for adoption?"

Wes crouched next to Bubba and scratched his neck. When Angel and the terriers came back, Posy's dog scooted under his knees, dropped the ball and bared her teeth at the terriers. They backed off and Angel laid the ball down between her front paws.

"I had five different foster placements in six years. I don't even remember them all. I used to worry they'd move me somewhere Deacon couldn't find me. Or that he'd realize all these other people were right and he wouldn't want me, either. That's all I had when I was a kid. Deacon. He wanted me when nobody else did."

Posy crouched next to him, her skirt tucked over her knees. "That's all anybody really needs, right? One person who wants them."

"I'm Bubba's person. Pep or not."

Posy stood. "Angel's an anarchist," she said. "I've been reading that site Travis told me about. All this time, I thought she was badly behaved when really she's been bored out of her mind. She wanted a job. She likes to spend part of each day engaging in bold action against squirrels, carpenter ants, Chloe Chastain and my mother's mail carrier."

"What did the mail carrier do to get on the list? Steal the coupons out of the grocery circular?"

"Maybe he nabs my mom's *People* magazine when Jennifer Aniston is on the cover. I don't know what his crime is, but Angel does." She watched Angel taunt the Lab with the tennis ball for a few seconds. "Did you know they have agility leagues for dogs? It's like obstacle courses with all these complicated tricks—the dogs have to be smart, fast and agile. I bet Angel would ace an agility course."

"You should get her in a class."

"She's not my dog," Posy said, but the statement didn't have nearly the force it usually did.

Angel carried the ball all the way back to the gate of the dog park, leaving the Lab frustrated behind her.

Posy clicked the button on her key ring to unlock her car.

"I thought I was the only one in Kirkland who locked the car," Wes said.

"Habit," she answered. "I haven't lived here in a long time."

Again, it was time for her to leave and he didn't want to see her go. He reached for her hand.

"After I drop Bubba off, I'm free. Can we meet for dinner?"

"Downtown?"

"Wherever you want."

"I'll be at my mom's."

"How does pizza sound?"

"Perfect."

When he got to her mom's house later, he parked in the driveway and then rang the doorbell. They didn't actually get to the pizza until long after it had gone cold, but he didn't mind.

Living with ballplayers as long as he had, cold pizza was practically its own food group.

SHE WOKE UP the next morning, groping on the nightstand for her phone before she was fully awake enough to realize it was ringing. Wes's arm slid around her from behind, cupping her breast. His erection pressed against her and she wished she'd woken up all the way so she could have let the phone go to voice mail.

"Hello?"

"Posy, the cops are here," Maddy said. "They arrested your mom."

CHAPTER SIXTEEN

FOR ONE SECOND she closed her eyes and allowed herself to press back, sinking into Wes's strong arms. Remembering the way she'd felt last night.

Then she rolled forward and sat up in bed.

"Where are they taking her?" she asked Maddy.

"It was the Kirkland P.D. Downtown, I guess."

"Tell her I'll be there as soon as I can."

Her shirt was on the floor next to the bed and she bent to grab it, acutely aware of her naked body. As soon as he found out her mom had been arrested, his loyalty to Deacon would trump the fragile relationship they'd built. This blow to the foundation's reputation was also the death blow to her hopes. She slid off the bed and crouched, pulling her shirt over her head even as she groped for her underwear.

He rolled to the edge of the bed and leaned over. His eyes were still half-closed, an invitation to come back to bed. She sat and pulled her pants on, hustling into them so she could be covered. Protected.

"Where are you going?"

"You need to go, Wes," she said.

"What's happening?"

"My mom's been arrested." She pushed herself up.

She couldn't face him, but she had to do it. He sat up, the sheet pulled around his waist, his chest and stomach bare and so beautiful, it was unfair. Even more unfair, she felt tears behind her eyes. "I don't know more than that."

"Posy, wait." He scrambled toward her, but she turned on her heel and left the room. She heard a bang as he stumbled into something in the room and a muffled curse. She went into the bathroom and started to brush her hair. The lock was broken, but she kept her heel wedged against the bottom of the door. She didn't want to have to face her anger.

He knocked, rattling the handle. "Posy, let me in."

"No. I'm not decent."

"I'm…we just… There's nothing I haven't seen."

She pulled her hair into a ponytail and secured it with a band. Her toothbrush was just out of reach and she stretched for it, trying to grab it with the tips of her fingers while keeping her foot against the door. She slipped and the door flew open, the handle banging hard into the tile wall. Wes leaned in the doorway, jeans open at his waist.

"We didn't do this, Posy." He shook his head. "I talked to Deacon last week and we agreed."

"I didn't think he would." It didn't make much difference who had caused the arrest.

"It was Chloe," he said. "It has to be."

"How can Chloe press charges? My mom didn't steal her money."

Wes straightened up, leaning one shoulder against the

door frame. "All the donors were legally victims. Chloe didn't just collect money, she donated some of her own."

"Oh, for the love of…" Posy threw her hairbrush into the sink. "What am I supposed to do now?"

Wes took a step toward her. "She needs a lawyer. I asked Deacon if we could help, if it came to this, but our lawyers can't represent her. If you need to find someone, we can get a referral."

She put the tube of toothpaste down. "You asked your brother if the Fallon Foundation lawyers could help my mom when she got arrested because she stole from you?"

He shrugged. "Stupid, I know."

She went to him and leaned against his chest. "Not stupid. Sweet. Well, maybe stupid, but also sweet." She kissed his jaw. "Thank you." He didn't want to have to choose between them. It was sweet, but it wasn't going to work.

He cupped her face, rubbing his thumbs along her chin and across her lips. "I want to help."

HE DRESSED AS QUICKLY as he could and met Posy by the front door. She was piling things into the huge bag she carried. A granola bar, several bottles of water, her phone, a package of tissues and a bottle of hand lotion. He stopped counting and just watched her. She talked a good game about giving up on her mom, but here she was, ready to go to bat the second Trish needed her.

She had her keys in one hand and the bag in the other, so he opened the door and held it for her. He felt a swish against his ankle and then heard Posy yell, "Damn it, Angel! No!"

The dog was gone, across the street and around the blue house.

"I'm so sorry," he said. "I wasn't thinking."

Posy shook her head. "She better keep far away from Chloe's house. The last thing I need is to give her another reason to come after us."

He held her coffee cup while she unlocked her car and then leaned down to kiss her. She'd been in the bathroom for less than five minutes and looked gorgeous.

"I'm right behind you," he said.

She pulled out and he watched until she made the turn at the end of the block. He walked to his own truck and then saw Chloe jogging toward him from her house across the street.

"They arrested Trish this morning," she said. "I know the fundraiser bank account was empty for at least a week, maybe longer, while she was supposed to have control of the money. I don't know what she did with it, but that check Posy gave you came from some other source."

Wes didn't know what to say. He wasn't going to lie to Chloe, but he wasn't about to give her any more details. He wondered who her source was at the bank. In a small town like this, it probably wasn't hard to find someone who knew someone who knew that kind of detail about a local account.

"I told you I had to protect my business," she went on. "I have a picture of you kissing Posy just now. If

I need it, I can use it. I'm the one who's obviously on the outside here. I raised money in good faith and I'm a victim just as much as anybody else."

"You don't have to threaten me, Chloe," he said.

"I'm taking care of my business because I have to. I can't see my name ruined over this. You and your brother should start thinking about your foundation and how you're going to protect yourselves."

He called Deacon from the truck on his way to the police station. He thought his brother was going to jump through the phone when he heard the story.

"This wasn't her call. She shouldn't have done this without talking to us—"

"I know, Deacon, believe me, I know," Wes said. And he did know. He was furious with Chloe. The trouble was, he also understood. She was protecting her family. They all were.

He pulled the truck over and parked. He was a block off Main Street in downtown Kirkland. The police station was two blocks north. There weren't many people out at this time of the morning, but the shops were starting to open and a park ranger was down on the public dock at the end of the street, unchaining the gates and picking up a few stray pieces of paper.

If he continued seeing Posy, would the Fallon Foundation lose the place they were building here in Kirkland? Deacon had been working on the Hand-to-Hand project for more than two years. They were so close now to seeing the program become reality.

"Where are you now?" Deacon asked.

"Parked downtown. I'm on my way to the station to help Posy with her mom."

His brother didn't say anything and the silence stretched between them.

"You don't want me to go," Wes said. It wasn't a question.

"It's not about what I want. What can we afford?"

"I told her I'd help."

"Vic contacted a local lawyer last week. Give his name to Posy. We can't take care of the bills for her, but Vic said he's good. He said since Trish Jones paid the money back and she doesn't have a record, she'll more than likely get a suspended sentence, especially because we're not pressing charges. This could all blow over in a week or two."

Posy couldn't walk into the police station alone. "I have to meet her, Deacon."

"Please, Wes, think about what you're doing. Are you sure what you and Posy have is the real thing? If you have any doubt, can you back off and let the lawyer take it?"

For the first time in his life, Wes wanted to turn his back on his brother. Just the idea made him feel like a worm. He had to stick with his family.

He called her cell but it went to voice mail. He texted her the name of the lawyer Vic had given them and then he drove back to his apartment.

Mrs. Meacham was asleep in her Adirondack chair in the yard. He sat in the chair next to her and stared at nothing for two hours. His phone didn't ring.

THE KIRKLAND POLICE DEPARTMENT was small. The university had a private police force that took care of the campus. That left very little in the way of a town. She was surprised at how run-down the small station was, with the mingled aroma of stale coffee, strong cleaning fluid and dust.

She could see her mother on the other side of a glass partition, being interviewed by a uniformed police officer and another man in a sport coat.

"Excuse me," Posy said to the officer behind the front desk. "That's my mother, Trish Jones, and I need to speak to her."

"She's being processed. You'll have to wait until she's through."

"But she doesn't have a lawyer. How can she be processed without her lawyer?"

The officer barely glanced at her. "She needs to ask for one. It's up to her."

Posy wanted to vault over the desk and crash through the back to get to her mom. She sat on the bench against the wall where the officer sent her and waited.

At first, she glanced out the front window every couple of seconds. Wes would be here soon. She'd be able to talk to him, to make a plan.

When fifteen minutes had passed and her mom was still in the back and there was still no sign of Wes, she pulled out her phone. No messages.

A few minutes later, her phone buzzed. She pressed the button and read his text. He wasn't coming. He and Deacon thought it best if he didn't show up at the police station. They'd found a lawyer, though, and here was the number. He'd signed it Wes. Just his name.

Posy dropped her phone into her purse.

He'd made his choice. Deacon and the obligation Wes felt to him trumped her. His brother would always come before everything else in Wes's life.

She was not going to cry in the Kirkland police station.

When Trish was finally released, the two of them collected her paperwork and Posy put the bail on her credit card. Grateful that no one was around to witness her mom's humiliation, she put her hand under her mother's elbow as they went down the steps outside and then realized she was treating her mom like an invalid when she was barely in her sixties. She dropped her hand.

Trish kept it together until she got to Posy's car. As soon as the doors were locked, though, she lost it. She cried, great heaving sobs.

Posy didn't know how to respond to her. "You stole the money, Mom," she said cautiously after a few moments. "It's not as if you got arrested for something you didn't do."

"But we paid it back."

"I paid it back."

Her mom jerked backward in her seat. "What is wrong with you?"

"You got arrested, Mom. That's what's wrong with me." And it meant she couldn't be with Wes.

"Please drop me back at the retreat center. I don't need help from you if you're going to be like this."

"How do you want me to be?" Posy asked. Her throat ached from holding back her tears all morning. She met her mom's eyes. "Tell me how you want me to be instead."

Trish pressed her lips together. "You're fine," she said. "The way you are is fine."

MADDY MET THEM at the desk and after they got Trish settled, she took Posy to her own room.

"What's going to happen?" she asked.

"I talked to a lawyer while she was at the station. He's going to take the case. Based on the facts I gave him, it's more than likely she'll get a suspended sentence. She's never been in trouble before and all the money was paid back on time."

"Oh, thank heavens for that." Maddy closed her eyes for a few seconds, and Posy knew she was praying. She wished she could think of what to pray for. There didn't seem to be a thing she knew she wanted that was also possible to have.

"What about you?" Maddy asked. "What are you going to do?"

"What I've been doing. The house is almost done and it's time to start on the store. I talked to my boss and he's fine if I stick around here until the end of the week. I'll have to see what happens with my mom after that."

"And Wes?"

"There's no more Wes."

Maddy tried to get her to share more, but Posy was too tired.

He called six times that morning and another six in the afternoon. Every hour and half hour, on the dot. She didn't answer. There wasn't anything to say.

WHEN SHE REFUSED to answer his calls or texts, Wes thought about driving to her house. But what was he going to say? *Sorry your mom got arrested. I can't do anything to help.*

He'd heard from Deacon, who told him Chloe was getting set to run a blog post dissociating herself from the fundraiser and dragging Trish and the Fallon Foundation through the mud. Vic had convinced her to hold off until the next morning, but they didn't have any way to shut her down.

He went for a run, hoping to clear his mind, but he didn't get any closer to a solution. The problem was he understood Chloe's position. She was doing what she thought was right to protect her business and her income. Once she found out about the theft, she almost had an obligation to make the facts public. She had to protect her image.

He slowed down. Her *image.*

That was the main issue for Chloe. She had to maintain her reputation. Her blog was built on her online persona, so she had to maintain it.

He picked up speed as excitement flooded him. What if there was a way to not only salvage her reputation, but to improve it? Set her up as someone who'd been through a challenging experience and who could be seen as an authority?

THE DOORBELL RANG around nine o'clock. Angel ran for the door, barking furiously. Posy looked out the window and then grabbed Angel before she opened it.

"Chloe?"

Chloe's hair and makeup were as flawless as usual. She folded her hands and gave Angel a glare before saying, "I know you probably don't want to talk to me and I don't blame you. I thought I should tell you, though, that I've worked out a deal with the Fallons. I can't drop the charges against your mom, but I'll do everything I can to see that she's treated fairly."

"Why?" Posy asked. Angel struggled in her arms. The last thing she wanted was to invite the other woman in, but she didn't want the dog to escape. She held the door open wider and backed up. "Come in, if you don't mind."

Chloe stepped just far enough inside to let the storm door close behind her. Posy put Angel on the ground and the little dog immediately retreated to the next room where she stood, growling.

"Wes put a proposal together," Chloe said. "The Fallon Foundation is going to sponsor a series of posts on my blog so we can teach other bloggers how to partner with nonprofits safely and legally. He lined up a series of experts—lawyers, marketers, an accountant. When the series is finished, I'm going to write a handbook and the Fallon centers will develop a workshop curriculum."

Posy put one hand behind her and leaned against the wall. "He put all that together today?"

"He seems intent on protecting your mom." Chloe

shook her head. "I had planned a fairly damning post for tomorrow, which I'm going to delete when I get home. I promised him I'd stop by. He's been trying to call you, but can't get through."

Angel growled again and Posy faced her, glad for the disruption. "Go to your bed."

The dog stood her ground for a second, but then reluctantly turned away.

"She listened to you."

"We've been practicing." Posy turned back. "What does this mean for my mom?"

"It means I'm not going to throw her to the wolves on my blog. I hope the issue will stay local and that the deal for a suspended sentence will go through."

Posy was so surprised that they'd been able to salvage anything from this mess and so deeply grateful that Chloe had agreed to the plan, that she said, "Thank you," and she meant it sincerely. "I'm sorry that my mom was irresponsible with the money. I wish this had never happened."

Chloe crossed her arms on her chest. "It's all working out fine in the end."

Fine, except Wes was staying here in Kirkland and she wasn't.

The other woman opened the storm door and walked onto the porch. "Good night," she said.

Posy lifted her hand. "Thanks again, Chloe."

She watched as Chloe crossed the street and walked up her own driveway. They were never going to be friends, not with the years of animosity and competition between them, but that was all right. Chloe was getting what she needed and Trish's deal would more than likely be okay.

She needed to thank Wes, but she thought she might cry if she heard his voice. A couple days. She needed a few days and then she'd be able to handle talking to him without thinking about what-ifs.

DEACON DROVE UP for the meeting with the town board. The waiver passed in a unanimous vote. The Hand-to-Hand program was a go.

Jay made a speech after the vote. He said that Kirkland was proud to stand with the Fallon Foundation. He touched on the fundraiser without getting into specifics, and then moved right on to welcoming the Hand-to-Hand program to town.

Ryan stayed behind and Wes introduced him to Deacon.

"Ten bucks you're the one who wrote that speech for the mayor," Wes said.

Ryan wiggled his hand back and forth. "Wrote it? Not quite. I did explain the finer points of what went on to Jay and helped him to see how we might want to discuss it in public."

Wes shook Ryan's hand. "I appreciate that. You made us look good in a situation a hair on the sketchy side."

"Ryan is a big fan of the Fallon centers," Deacon said. "As soon as you start filling jobs, you should ask this guy for his résumé."

Ryan grinned. "The center's going to have to field

a rec-league team. That's the only reason you're trying to poach me from the mayor's office."

"On second thought," Wes said, "forget about applying. We need somebody who can actually play defense." He tried to ignore the sick feeling he got every time he thought about his new job and all the ways he was being tied more tightly to this town. He wished he could have shared this with Posy, but that was impossible.

CHAPTER SEVENTEEN

IN THE END she didn't have to have a going-out-of-business sale at Wonders. She started to write an ad, intending to put it in the regional papers, but then remembered her mom's blog. The stupid thing had started all this trouble. Maybe it could help her out here at the end. She wrote a quick blog about the store closing and posted it. Then she remembered that Trish had a database of customers who'd been shopping at Wonders for years. She brought her laptop out to the deck and sent a note about the sale to the mailing list.

Her in-box was immediately inundated with notes from customers begging Trish to keep the store open. Mixed with the flood of Oh No! messages was one marked with a red Urgent flag. The subject line read, Read this before you hold the sale.

The email was from a woman named Emily Weaver. She and her daughters ran a Christmas shop near the Canadian border. She'd been trying for years to get a commission from the man who made the nativity sets her mother sold, but he had a waiting list and she wasn't going to get any for that holiday season. She told Posy she would pay almost double the wholesale price for the nativity sets Trish currently had in stock.

Posy replied and told her she could have the nativity sets, but only if she agreed to take either the snow globes or the nutcrackers. She'd barely hit Send when the reply came back with an agreement for the snow globes.

The next urgent message came from a man who had a chain of model-train stores in northern Pennsylvania. He said he'd take Trish's entire inventory of miniatures off her hands, but only if he was allowed to pack it himself. She sent him back a list of what she had on hand and he sent her back a price. Posy cross-checked it against the wholesale prices and figured that even though it was a little low, her mom would not only get rid of all the miniatures, she'd get paid for every one of them. If they held a retail sale, she couldn't hope for that kind of return. Posy wasn't sure exactly what she was supposed to object to in terms of packing the boxes, a job she certainly didn't want, so she told him he was welcome to come.

The line of hand-painted German ornaments and individually signed Advent calendars went next. Another email came through with a buyer for the nutcrackers. Before the day was over, Posy had agreements for three-quarters of the stock in the store. Her mom's apparently excellent taste had paid off. Who knew the objects crammed into Wonders were almost all exclusive and almost all worth something to someone?

Once she was down to odds and ends and small lots of unique items, she sent another note to the mailing list letting them know the sale was canceled, but offering holiday surprise packages at a set rate of twenty dollars each, plus shipping. She took orders for a hundred packages and then told the list the stock was sold out. She might end up with some leftover items, but she didn't feel up to fussing with the details. She'd donate anything she couldn't ship out.

She called a few moving companies and found one that would send a crew to Wonders to pack the surprise packages for shipping. All the merchandise was being picked up by the buyers or their representatives on Saturday, so by Sunday morning, the Wonders of Christmas Shoppe could close its doors for good. Posy would be able to pay her aunt back and have a little left over to apply to the second mortgage she'd taken out.

ON SATURDAY MORNING, Emily, the woman from upstate, came for the nativity sets on the dot of nine o'clock, along with her two daughters. Posy was waiting for her outside Wonders with Angel on her leash. When the van pulled up, she unlocked the door of the store.

The cinnamon scent was still strong, but the place looked a little neglected. She closed the door behind her and let Angel off her leash. The dog leaped up into the front-window display, which had always been her home base when she came to work with Trish.

"I'll get some lights on and then we can pack them up."

Posy had a bag of packing supplies, tape, markers, labels and some bungee cords, but Emily had her own boxes and she and her daughters made short work of the packing. They were barely out the door when the crew she'd hired from the moving company showed up and then the man from Pennsylvania who wanted the miniatures.

She kept the dismantling organized and everyone was working carefully, but she was still on edge. As much as she'd looked forward to this day, it felt wrong. Or, maybe not wrong, but sad. Lonely? After this, she'd have no more tether to Kirkland.

That had always been her dream, but that dream had started to seem tarnished. For one thing, she had no idea what she was going to do with Angel. She walked over to the front window and spotted the dog sitting amidst the remains of a display that had been taken apart and separated into surprise boxes.

Angel wasn't the type of pet who could be put up for adoption. Some poor family would think they were getting a standard, garden-variety schnoodle. Instead, they'd be living with a fluffy, white hell beast.

She'd started working with Angel on some basic commands and the dog was doing well, but knowing how to sit on command wasn't going to change her basic nature.

Posy snapped her fingers and Angel trotted over to be picked up. She didn't always enjoy snuggling, but there were times when Angel was content to pretend to be a lapdog. There were also times when Posy was happy to have a lapdog.

She traveled too much to have a dog.

Someone knocked on the door. She was still holding Angel when she greeted the man standing on the sidewalk. "I'm Mitchell," he said. "We made arrangements about the nutcrackers."

She stepped back to let him past her into the store, but he held his hand out. "It's very nice to meet you, Posy."

"You, too."

He was looking at her more intently than was comfortable, so she shifted the dog in front of her. Angel would bite him if he made a wrong move, she was positive. He let her hand go, though, and looked through the window at the store. "So this is Wonders. Is Trish here?"

"No," Posy said. "She's on a retreat."

"I see." Mitchell had parked a big silver Cadillac at the curb and he returned to it to pull some plastic bins out of the back.

She picked up one of the bins and led him inside the store to show him where the nutcrackers were stored. There was a display on the main floor and then several cartons in the storeroom in the back.

Mitchell didn't say much as they worked, but Posy caught him watching her a few times. She didn't feel entirely comfortable being alone in the store with him, so she wound up putting Angel on her leash and taking her for a walk.

When they got back, he was tying the trunk of his car down with a bungee cord. "Thank you, Posy," he said. "You've done a wonderful job. Your mom must be grateful after all she's been through."

"She's doing just fine." Posy didn't know what he'd heard about her mom or how, but she didn't feel like stretching the conversation out just to dig for details.

"I've been out of the town," he said, apropos of nothing. "I have a country home in France. It's quite nice, but remote. No internet or cell service. I like it that way. I saw your message about the sale the day I landed in New York. I'm glad I didn't miss it."

"Me, too," Posy said. She wasn't sure why he was telling her all this, but she hoped if she agreed with him he'd move along.

He held his hand out again. "Very nice meeting you."

She shook his hand and then watched while he went around to the driver's side of his car. She wasn't sure the bungee cords were going to hold, but he seemed to think the ropes were secure.

As she was checking out the trunk, his license plate registered, "Dr. Train."

Mitchell. Mitch.

She banged on the trunk and then motioned for him to roll down the window.

"You're Mitch from Mitch's Train Yard, aren't you?"

"I am." This time when he smiled, it was a genuinely delighted grin. "I didn't know how much your mom told you about me. I didn't want to ruin the surprise if you didn't know about our plans."

She felt ridiculous. What was she supposed to do now? Ask him what those plans were?

"My intentions are completely honorable," he said, reading her mind. "Your mother is the light of my life."

"I don't think she should move to Ohio right away," Posy said.

Mitch rubbed the tip of his nose with his index finger as he considered that. "I'm going to leave it up to your mom. What do you say?"

What could she say? It was what she'd wanted all along. Her mom, making independent decisions. If she was going to let her mother clean up her own mistakes, she was going to have to let her make them in the first place. Although she'd proved overly adept at that in the past.

"I memorized your license plate," she said. "And I've got your email and cell phone info from the sale."

"Excellent," Mitch said. "It was nice meeting you."

Posy had no idea if he was insane, creepy or one of the gentlest people she'd ever met. She would have to let her mom make that call.

She and Angel went back inside the store.

Thick dust was gathered on some of the display shelves and the floors desperately needed to be swept now that all the clutter was gone. She'd brought cleaning supplies with her, but faced with the huge empty space, she couldn't find the motivation.

She was leaving. The house was on the market, Wonders was closed, her mom was on probation and might be staying at the retreat center or might be heading off with her surgeon. All Posy had to do was figure out a plan for Angel and she was free and clear.

She felt like crying.

She missed Wes.

"Angel," she called. "Let's go." The dog leaped off the window seat and skidded to a stop in front of her. They'd been working on some of the basic commands at night. Angel was a fast learner, especially when there were biscuits involved. Posy clipped the leash on the collar and straightened just as the door opened.

Wes.

"You're really leaving?"

"The last ornament got boxed up not twenty minutes ago. Now I just have to figure out what to do about Angel and I'm on my way."

He hadn't come all the way into the store—instead he was half in the front door, holding it propped open with his elbow and heel.

"You're giving Angel away?"

Posy tightened her grip on the leash. "I can't keep her. You saw how I live."

"But you…"

He'd been about to say, "But you love Angel," but he couldn't finish the sentence. She did love Angel, he knew that. The same way he knew she loved him.

"I'm going to miss you, Posy," he said. "It won't be the same without you here." He'd practiced saying that. He didn't want to make a fool of himself or embarrass either one of them by fumbling around looking for words. He'd wanted to say goodbye and that was done.

She shrugged. All of a sudden, Angel gave a loud bark and lunged to the end of her leash. Posy's grip must have been loose because the leash slipped out of her hand, whipping behind Angel as the dog bolted for the entrance.

"Shut the door!" Posy yelled, but he couldn't slam it because Angel was on her way through and he was afraid he'd crush her. He tried to step on the leash but it slid past too quickly and then the dog was gone.

Posy was running toward him and then they heard the screech of brakes outside and a high-pitched yelp. Then nothing.

He was back in Madrid, only this time the truck missed him and hit the dog. This time it wasn't him being flung across the street, it was Angel.

Posy stopped short, her hands over her mouth. "Oh, God, Wes. Did she get hit? I can't look. I can't look."

He couldn't see. There was a knot of people in the street now, standing around a black SUV that was stopped in the middle of the road. He didn't see Angel no matter how hard he looked for her to come racing toward him.

"I don't see her."

"I can't go out there," Posy said, but she walked up to him, put her hand on the doorjamb and then went out and down the step to the sidewalk.

He caught up to her and put his arm across her shoulders. She picked up the pace as they got closer to the people gathered in the road. "Excuse me," she said to a woman standing at the back of the crowd. He heard her voice, shaky in a way he'd never have expected from Posy and he stepped in front of her.

"I'll do this, Posy. You wait here."

Her eyes filled with tears. "No. We'll go together. Okay?"

He took her hand. It had been too long. If Angel hadn't been killed, someone would have been running for help, for a vet, for blankets, for something. He cleared a path and the two of them moved through the crowd and then suddenly they were in an open space. Angel was lying on the road, the leash limp behind her. A teenage girl knelt near her, sobbing.

"I didn't see her. She came out of nowhere."

A man was coming from the other side of the crowd with a blanket.

Wes and Posy made their way over to the small body.

"Damn it," Posy whispered. "I wasn't going to give you away. I was just talking."

Wes took the blanket from the man and knelt next to Posy. She reached out and stroked the dog's head.

"Wes, she's still breathing," Posy said.

She was right. The dog's sides were moving up and down steadily. Now that he was paying attention, he didn't see any blood, either.

He grabbed his phone out of his pocket. "We need a vet."

A woman stepped forward. "There's one around the corner, next to the old post office on Brand Street."

SHE DIDN'T REMEMBER exactly how they got to the vet. Wes carried Angel, she knew that. They ran. She remembered being glad she was wearing her sneakers. The two of them were side by side when they got to the vet's office and they were side by side when the doctor examined Angel.

They were side by side when the dog woke up and

bit the nurse who was trying to trim the fur away from a cut on her foreleg.

The doctor shooed them out of the examining room while the nurse called for help with Angel.

Posy burst into tears and flung herself at Wes.

"I wasn't going to give her away. I wouldn't. I couldn't."

He wrapped his arms around her. "I know."

"I'm not giving you up, either." She held him tight. "If you have to live here, I'll figure it out. I promise. I'll learn how to live here. It's not too late, right? Wes?"

He was shaking his head.

He couldn't be shaking his head. Not now, not when she'd finally realized that she couldn't let him go.

"Don't shake your head, Wes. We can figure this out. You don't take no for an answer, don't say it to me."

"I'm saying no to Kirkland, Posy. You'd be miserable here and so would I."

He pushed on her shoulder and the two of them shuffled a few steps to the right where they could look through a glass panel into the room where Angel was being worked on.

"We don't belong in Kirkland, Posy. Not you. Not me. Not Angel."

"But your brother…"

Wes took a deep breath. "I owe him, but I guess I've always been afraid he was finally going to wise up and not want me around." He tightened his hand on her shoulder. "You taught me that you can't keep people tied to you with a debt like that. Deacon's fine and I will be, too. I will be, if we're together, that is."

She kissed him. Or maybe he kissed her. It didn't matter who started it, she knew for sure that neither of them ended it for a good long time. Neither of them wanted to let go. That was just the way they were made.

HE KEPT HIS ARM around her shoulders while they sat in the waiting-room chairs. The doctor wanted to keep Angel for a few hours for observation, but he was confident she was as good as new.

"Maybe the accident knocked some manners into her," Posy said, but she didn't sound as if she had much hope. Especially since the nurse had walked past with a thick, white bandage on her thumb.

He called his brother.

"Deacon?" Posy's hand covered his on her shoulder. "It's Wes. I have to talk to you about that job."

"Oh, for Pete's sake," Deacon said. "You'd think after ten years I'd learn. But I don't. I'm an idiot."

Wes was confused. "D.?"

"You're turning it down, right?"

"Right, but—"

"Julia bet me you were going to say no. And now I have to take her to see Barry Manilow, who is still touring for some reason I can't understand." Wes heard a muffled thump. He thought his brother might have kicked something. "You owe me. I was getting a weekend in Vegas if I won."

"You're not angry?"

"Angry? I'm screwed. I have to sit through a *Barry Manilow* concert."

"But about the job. You're not angry that I said no?"

"No." Deacon paused. "Should I be?"

"No," Wes said.

And that was what it felt like to be free.

"Wait, maybe *you* should take Julia to the Barry Manilow concert. It's your fault I lost the bet."

"I know better than to bet against Julia."

"You probably like Barry Manilow, though."

Posy was looking at him and he smiled. She smiled back and he thought he'd never seen anything as pretty. Her face was streaked with tears. There was dirt on her shirt where she'd wiped her hands after kneeling in the road. She was perfect.

"Let me ask Posy and I'll get back to you."

POSY VETOED Barry Manilow, but she convinced Julia that the four of them should go to Vegas. The Hotel Marie had a beautiful property there and she got them a gorgeous suite. None of them told Deacon that it was International Karaoke Week until the plane touched down. And by that time, it was too late for him to make his escape.

Late on their third night, Wes and Posy, wearing the third-place duet medals they'd won in a competition that night, found themselves outside the Little Wedding Chapel.

Wes put his arm around Posy's shoulders. "What do you think?" he asked.

Her pulse jumped. She couldn't help it. She was outside a Vegas wedding chapel with Wes. But he wasn't proposing. He wouldn't. Not when they'd barely finished moving Wes into his own pet-friendly apartment around the corner from her condo in Rochester. He and Deacon were finalizing plans for Wes to take a fundraising position with the Fallon Foundation. Posy was continuing in her work with the Hotel Marie, but she'd begun sketching out a career plan that would allow her to cut back on her travel in a year or two and move into management.

"What do I think about what?"

"Couple years, you and me, right back here."

She put her hand across his chest and smiled up at him. "Here cleaning up at International Karaoke Week or here…"

"Here at the chapel. Fallon and Jones, together forever."

She squeezed him and smiled again. "My mom would kill me if I didn't let her plan my wedding." He tipped his head down toward her and she kissed him. "But the Fallon and Jones part sounds exactly right."

In a few years, he did ask her to marry him, and she did say yes. They had the wedding in Milton on the grounds of the very first Fallon Community Center. Trish planned the entire thing (although Posy chose her own dress), and every detail was perfect, right down to the theme…Christmas in July.

* * * * *

REQUEST YOUR FREE BOOKS!
2 FREE NOVELS PLUS 2 FREE GIFTS!

Harlequin

Super Romance

Exciting, emotional, unexpected!

What happens when a Texas nanny learns she is the biological daughter of a prince? Her rancher boss steps in to help protect her from the paparazzi, but who can protect her from her attraction to him?

Read on for an excerpt of
A HOME FOR NOBODY'S PRINCESS
by USA TODAY bestselling author Leanne Banks.

Available October 2012

"This is out of control." Benjamin sighed. "Well, damn. I guess I'm gonna have to be your fiancé."

Coco's jaw dropped. "What?"

"It won't be real," he said quickly, as much for himself as for her. After the debacle of his relationship with Brooke, the idea of an engagement nearly gave him hives. "It's just for the sake of appearances until the insanity dies down. This way it won't look like you're all alone and ready to have someone take advantage of you. If someone approaches you, then they'll have to deal with me, too."

She frowned. "I'm stronger than I seem," she said.

"I know you're strong. After what you went through for your mom and helping Emma to settle down, I know you're strong. But it's gotta be damn tiring to feel like you've always got to be on guard."

Coco sighed and her shoulders slumped. "You're right about that." She met his gaze with a wince. "Are you sure you don't mind doing this?"

"It's just for a little while," he said. "You mentioned that a fiancé would fix things a few minutes ago. I had to run it through my brain. It seems like the right thing to do."

She gave a slow nod and bit her lip. "Hmm. But it would cut into your dating time."

Benjamin laughed. "That's not a big focus at the moment."

"It would be a huge relief for me," she admitted. "If you're sure you don't mind. And we'll break it off the second you feel inconvenienced."

"No problem," he said. "I'll spread the word. Should be all over the county by lunchtime. No one can know the truth. That's the only way this will work."

Coco took a deep breath and closed her eyes as if preparing to take a jump into deep water. "Okay" she said, and opened her eyes. "Let's do it."

Will Coco be able to carry out the charade?

Find out in Leanne Banks's new novel—
A HOME FOR NOBODY'S PRINCESS.

Available October 2012 from Harlequin® Special Edition®

Sometimes love strikes in the most unexpected circumstances...

Soon-to-be single mom Antonia Wright isn't looking
for romance, especially from a cowboy. But when
rancher and single father Clayton Traub rents a room
at Antonia's boardinghouse, Wright's Way, she isn't
prepared for the attraction that instantly sizzles between
them or the pain she sees in his big brown eyes.
Can Clay and Antonia trust their hearts and build the
family they've always dreamed of?

Don't miss

THE MAVERICK'S
READY-MADE FAMILY

by Brenda Harlen

celebrating 15 YEARS

Love Inspired

Another heartwarming installment of

— TEXAS TWINS —

Two sets of twins, torn apart by family secrets,
find their way home

When big-city cop Grayson Wallace visits an elementary
school for career day, he finds his heartstrings
unexpectedly tugged by a six-year-old fatherless boy and
his widowed mother, Elise Lopez. Now he can't get the
struggling Lopezes off his mind. All he can think about
is what family means—especially after discovering
the identical twin brother he hadn't known he had
in Grasslands. Maybe a trip to ranch country is just
what he, Elise and little Cory need.

Look-Alike Lawman
by Glynna Kaye

Available October 2012
wherever books are sold.

www.LoveInspiredBooks.com

LI87770

At their grandmother's request, three estranged
sisters return home for Christmas to the small town
of Beckett's Run. Little do they know that this family
reunion will reveal long-buried secrets…
and new-found love.

Discover the magic of Christmas in a brand-new
Harlequin® Romance miniseries.

In October 2012, find yourself
SNOWBOUND IN THE EARL'S CASTLE
by **Fiona Harper**

Be enchanted in November 2012 by a
SLEIGH RIDE WITH THE RANCHER
by **Donna Alward**

And be mesmerized in December 2012 by
MISTLETOE KISSES WITH THE BILLIONAIRE
by **Shirley Jump**

Available wherever books are sold.

HARLEQUIN

Blaze™

red-hot reads

**Two sizzling fairy tales with men
straight from your wildest dreams...**

Fan-favorite authors
Rhonda Nelson & Karen Foley
bring readers another installment of

Blazing Bedtime Stories, Volume IX

THE EQUALIZER

Modern-day righter of wrongs, Robin Sherwood is a man
on a mission and will do everything necessary to see that
through, especially when that means catching
the eye of a fair maiden.

GOD'S GIFT TO WOMEN

Sculptor Lexi Adams decides there is no such thing as the
perfect man, until she catches sight of Nikos Christakos,
the sexy builder next door. She convinces herself that she
only wants to sculpt him, but soon finds a cold stone
statue is a poor substitute for the real deal.

Available October 2012 wherever books are sold.